TAKE CREEK, FOR EXAMPLE

by

Chris Rugeley

7.13 Books

Printed in the United States of America

First Edition
1 2 3 4 5 6 7 8 9

Excerpts of this novel appeared in *The Florida Review*.

Cover art by Madeleine Tonzi
Edited by Leland Cheuk

Library of Congress Cataloging-in-Publication Data

ISBN (paperback): 979-8-9877471-0-0
ISBN (eBook): 979-8-9877471-1-7
LCCN: 2023940661

For Abby

PART ONE

THE FALL

1

LOUD, LEAN JERSEY LANDER came charging up the path out of the trees into the glaring yellowsalt sun. His body arched forward, just so, all legs, long-stepping, with his hands twitching loosely at his sides. Over his shoulder, he carried a large plastic tote bag full of crab apples, which seemed to cause him some mild discomfort as he walked. He waved at me with his elbows and laughed. Like always, I would pretend not to notice him until he was standing pretty much right next to me.

Such was the cadence of our friendship. It denoted all the things we had grown to expect.

Jersey was hands down the wildest, most talented sculptor at Take Creek, but his temper kept getting in the way, like a block between his heart and his work. One moment, he would be in The Zone shaping some new lurid piece, then out of nowhere he would just snap, falling to his muses, and go completely off-the-rails berserk. He would throw a chair, or break a bottle, or tear apart a ream of paper and light it on fire by the dumpsters. It didn't matter what the thing was—Jersey Lander had it out for the raging.

I did what I could. I tried to be there for him. Nothing was easy, though, especially when it came to being there for other people. Being there for other people was like losing a war over and over and still racing back to the frontlines to get slaughtered.

It tasted like metal.

It smelled like burning plastic.

That morning, I sat quietly under a tree off The Quad, taking photographs of The Chow Hall, breaking it down into its parts. It was another one of Salter's rogue assignments about the sanctity of objects, but mostly I loved it. Jersey materialized a few feet away and dropped his bag on the still-damp grass. His breath reeked of bad milky coffee, and he moaned in exhaustion, humming a tune by Moniker, his favorite band. Today, he sported a ratty, red thermal tee, black gum-soled boots, and tactical ripstop overalls whose left side pocket had been designed uniquely for a framing square. Any minute now he would take stock of his various ideations. I became suddenly interested to know what he was up to next.

Jersey zeroed in on the apple in his hand, spotted gold and yolky, a bruised piece. He spun it carefully with the tips of his fingers, then threw it at the tree and shrieked.

"Take Creek is a racket," he said. "I should've gone to RISD or Yale. I should've done New York. I should've checked out Los Angeles."

"Salter says pain is the beginning," I said. "It's where process takes over. You have to keep pushing."

Jersey rolled his eyes and flipped me the bird. Maybe he had a point there, or something.

We were twenty-two and just beginning our senior year. All of us were stuck on the question why. Every occurrence seemed to have a weight to it, an undefined purpose, a brooding exception for something we forgot. Jersey even had two spindly gray hairs above his left ear, which lent him this added intensity.

"Have you heard about the new transfer?" he said.

"He goes by Manning," I said. "That's all I know."

"I heard he's coming from Europe."

"Sure, Jersey."

"Southern Europe. Island Europe. The blue sea. The olive tree. The white marble stairs in the foyer."

"Listen to you," I said.

"The fisherman there smokes endless cigarettes," Jersey said. "The cask pours an earthy vintage, and the halls are bursting with work by the old masters."

I looked at him, a cautious stare.

"Franny says we should pay attention or we'll get swallowed up," I said.

"Your girlfriend can be so dramatic," Jersey said, waving me off.

"I'm serious. We have to be careful. This isn't just another one of your jokes."

"What if it is? What then?"

"Franny knows," I said. "She has a tendency to see things. She can render the form of certain events before they even happen."

Jersey laughed and coughed at the same time. He flashed me a look like I was talking out of my foot. He had one of those sharp, impassioned faces, with a big pointed triangle of a nose and these perilously sunken brown eyes. He hailed from New Jersey, a place called West Orange, where his parents ran a world-renowned art gallery that had a really long Wikipedia page.

West Orange was fine, Jersey liked to tell me, but he had other plans. When he left there he vowed to never move back, not even if someone paid him, though he knew it wasn't likely anyone would.

"Do you want to get some chow now?" I said. "Or would you rather we wait out the rush?"

Jersey didn't answer. He stood and looked down at me and grabbed another apple and threw it at the tree, pointing at the core as it tumbled onto the grass.

"Shoot that," he said, and screamed.

There was something beautiful about Jersey when he lashed out like that, something I thought I wanted. The way his thick curly mop blew in the breeze. The way his body cast a slantwise shadow on the lawn. The poor apple. The madness of sculpture. It was the stuff of film, sound and vision, the work of a real gutsy genius.

Here he was on camera, the starving young artist with slender dainty hands, screaming murder at the world, grabbing apples two at a time, and throwing them at a tree off The Quad.

Blown out.

Awake to the texture of things.

2

TAKE CREEK SAT ON this sprawling woodsy campus, way upstate, buried in the pines, miles from any city. We were committed to a credo, a set of modest but binding principles. Enrollment was somewhere around two hundred fifty. Tuition crept up on sixty grand a year. We ran a small dairy, a foundry, a hatchery, a theater. We printed zines. We sold produce to the co-op in town. We stitched up the holey clothes however we wanted.

Many of the buildings on campus dated back centuries, while others were afterthoughts, ad-hoc structures, and odd markers in the history of design. This gave the place a chaotic, unreasonable quality. We all knew it. We loved it well. Our workshops were held in outbuildings, sheds, escarpments of wood and lapsed material, a long-winded study of found objects. The Library was a geodesic dome, The Zone was a renovated barn, The Shaker was a concrete box modeled on an airplane hangar, and The Chow Hall had once been a tennis bubble. I did most of my work in a space called The Media Annex, an old Unitarian Church that had its own belfry, parsonage, and stable.

The farmers nearby, the neighbors, thought we were something like Maoists. Though I learned later what a Maoist really was, and we were nowhere close. Although Jersey did carry around a little red book in his back pocket, a cache of pages that he always kept blank, for reasons he would never explain.

The higher-ups referred to our credo as The Four Noble Pillars:

(1) Art

(2) Academics

(3) Labor

(4) Cooperative self-government

The Four Noble Pillars lent structure to our daily lives. They helped us make sense of the passing of time, however we happened to be passing it.

Everywhere we went we heard stories that gave us hope in these boundless, worldsick times. Alumni had gone on to win Pulitzers, Pritzkers, Nobels, Golden Lions, Genius Grants, the Palme D'Or. They had painted, sculpted, wrote, designed, installed, shot, and screened. Some taught at prestigious universities. Some curated shows at museums. Others ran foundations or occupied major seats in government. A few even headed multinational corporations—of these we would never speak.

We were miles from any city. The light turned severe. The food was organic. The weather swung to extremes and then some. We shoveled the snow ourselves when it fell. We lit candles in old cans of olive oil when the power went out.

Everything was perfect.

In the morning, we woke at these godawful hours, rising from the edge of sleep in The Barracks, stumbling around our bunks in total darkness, looking for a pair of dry woolen socks. We milked the cows. We tended to the goats. We fed the chickens and ducks and cleaned out their coops with apple cider vinegar. Most days we collected eggs in the same soggy cartons and brought them to The Chow Hall for breakfast at 7:30 a.m. sharp. Afterward there was an hour of free time. Then we went out and started our sessions.

Here we studied light patterns, or talked about Goya, or fixed tractors, or propagated plants. Some of us wrote freeform verse about long-dead Estonian anarchists in French. The curriculum was complicated. We were plenty unorthodox. For the average freshman, there was a real getting used to, a warming up, and it either happened, or it didn't. Attrition was the ruthless saw.

I was here for Salter. I had gotten in on a portfolio shot at a homeless camp in San Francisco, which was famous for such camps. Every summer I spent a few weeks there with my Uncle Mel, Aunt Madge, and their son, my cousin, Dax. The summer before applications were due, I was shooting a lot, roaming around the city, and building out this ragged and seedy aesthetic. The images were raw, stripped down, and shot in a soft, harrowing light. Much of the work was sexually explicit. The needles formed prickly mounds in the tree wells. Heroin was just about everywhere.

The first time I went to office hours, Salter sat in a chair by the window with the shades drawn. He had a woven blanket draped over his legs. A half-eaten bagel collected dust on his desk. Salter was overbearing, brown-eyed, and skeptical. He was always missing a few of his teeth. His books were stacked in disorderly piles on the shelves and the wooden floor. Hundreds of photographs were tacked to the wall behind his desk, like his life had been assembled into a collage. Above the file cabinet, next to the window, there was a poster of a skier falling off a cliff. In the bottom left, a small caption in bright blue letters read: FIND COLORADO. No one had a clue what that meant.

Salter drank red wine from a coffee mug as he flipped through my work. He said that Cindy Sherman, Garry Winogrand, and Larry Clark were to be my new heroes, so I should dress normal and act modest to blend in, to not stick out like the rest of them. He said I had promise, but that I needed to keep pushing. He said that one day I would understand what this meant.

I thanked him.

He nodded.

Then he said to get the fuck out of his office and to not come back until I had work worth spitting on.

That was my first day.

3

Franny Meyer had a barrel-cone spliff pinched permanently between her fingers. It always seemed to be half-smoked. She brandished it before her eyes like a wand. She wore all this transfuturistic makeup in Technicolor stripes and smudges across her face.

That was what she called it.

Transfuturistic.

No one had a clue what it meant.

Her hair was buzzed off but for two long braids at the top of her head. They dangled coolly and looked like tassels on a graduation hat.

Franny had come to Take Creek for post-postmodern dance, which meant she was here for Zoe. I never really knew what she was thinking, though. This was what I found most attractive about her. She stood apart, always in a landscape of her own devising. Plus she was really short and really small. Everything about her just sent me spinning. That was my thing. I couldn't explain it. I wasn't especially tall. It was just what I liked. The small quiet things moved me. I figured this was because everything else in life—the worldhum, the shutter, the sound of cool running water—everything else was already so loud and so big.

I plopped down on her bunk and put my hands on her legs, waving around the newest issue of *Sputum.*

"Are you selling news for some dead political party?" Franny said.

"This says you're the golden child of the dance world," I said.

"You're talking about *Sputum*."

"That's right," I said. "Zoe says you're the top dancer to come through Take Creek in fifteen years, and that you're in the top three of all time."

Franny shrugged.

"Come on," I said. "Zoe danced with the Bolshoi. She started rumors in Prague back when it was still in Czechoslovakia."

"I wouldn't get carried away," Franny said.

"Magda at *The Lancer* just wrote me about submitting new work," I said. "It looks like Salter dropped my name at a recent show. Who knows, Franny? It could be me next. Don't you think?"

"That magazine has a readership of probably twelve people."

"It's a zine," I said.

Franny laughed, and when Franny laughed she snorted. She scooted closer. I could feel myself getting warm there on the bed.

"You'll be famous," I said.

Franny looked at me.

"They'll name streets after you. They'll write books about your style. Someone will coin the term Frannyesque."

"I don't care about being famous," Franny said.

"Of course you do. We all do. Look at Jersey. He needs it so bad."

"This is different."

"You're no different," I said. "The exposure is nice. It's only natural to want recognition for your work."

"When Manning gets here, there won't be any more exposure," Franny said. "Not for me. Not for you. Not for Jersey. Not for anyone. It could get really weird here. Just try not to lose the magic."

Franny was my girlfriend for going on almost a year now. She had a tendency to see things. She could render the form of certain events before they even happened in the world. She drove this rusty silver Toyota pickup with a topper that leaked and a front axle that made an awful grinding sound whenever it was cranked too far to the right. In the backseat she kept three cardboard boxes full of cassette tapes, selections in classical, jazz, rock, rap, electronica, punk, outlaw country, blues, anything we could think of—we just named it. On weekends the two of us would drive around the countryside and listen to music and smoke spliffs for as long as we wanted. Then we would pull over and have this achingly slow, campy kind of sex, right up whatever dirt road was there, wherever it was we were going.

There was an awkward loftiness to our misunderstandings. We knew this. We were all right with this. We admired them more than a little.

4

MY MOTHER WAS FROM a country that was no longer on the map. She was always reminding me and my older brother Paul that we were lucky to be here at all. Magravia once bordered Romania to the east, Hungary to the west, and Ukraine to the north, but now it was gone, divvied up into irregular shapes for its neighbors. The names had all been changed, the lines redrawn. Nothing would ever be the same. During the war, after the invasion, thousands of people were put to death and burned in the cold basements of abandoned buildings. Women and children were raped and left to rot at the bend in the river. Entire families had been shot in their homes, just walking to church, hidden from view. Their bodies were buried in unmarked graves all over the countryside and people were still unearthing bodies today. Every so often they would find a new grave and for a few minutes it would become a headline.

I read about it in the news.

Sometimes I read about it.

Sometimes I just said yes when my mother asked if I read about it.

"It's so much horror," I would say to her. "It's so sick that no one cares about what happened."

Whenever it came up, Paul used to roll his eyes in this overly dramatic way and say that it didn't really matter now, though, did it?

This drove our mother to fits of rage. She would yell at Paul for hours, screaming in Magravian and slapping him for being such a thoughtless ingrate. Later Paul would corner me in the hall and hit me when no one was looking. He would say that I was a mouthbreather, and that art was for losers and swine, and that I should pick which of the two I liked most because I wasn't going anywhere fast anyway. Paul went on to study business at Midwestern State in Wichita Falls. He now owned four Subway franchises and was divorced from a woman twice his age.

Our father was South Texas to the bone, a lone star through and through. He grew up in a small town called Schulenburg and was the son of poor Czech farmers. He co-owned a roadside barbecue joint off the Beltway and believed that God created the world in much less than a week. He drove a medium Dodge, ate grits for breakfast, and smoked wooden-tip Black & Mild cigars in the backyard, pacing alone by the fence. He didn't care much about art, but he had integrity and he always kept the house stocked with paper and pencils, paints and supplies. I drew. I smeared. I collaged. I colored. I was the young boy at the table, working on his pictures. It didn't matter what they were. My father hung them on the walls of every room. He said that seeing my pictures there made it easier for him to get out of bed, especially on those mornings when he didn't even feel like opening his eyes.

We lived in this southwestern pocket of blown-out, suburban Houston. Our house sat on a cul-de-sac between a strip mall and the dump. Everyone I knew rode a one-speed bike. From my bedroom window I could see the signs for the Circle K and the Walmart. Across the street from our house, a limousine driver lived with his son. The man was Magravian, too, and on the weekends when they came over for dinner he would load his son and me into the backseat and drive us around the cul-de-sac over and over, until he finally stopped in front of our house and turned to look at us and, in a thick Magravian accent, said, "We've arrived at the Met, my little darlings. Now go on and have yourselves a ball."

To me, the limousine was a shaky notion, out of place yet somehow glaring. Then and there, I found myself attracted to this very strange question. It would be a few years before my parents gave me my first camera, but once it started I just knew that there would be no taking it back.

Quickly, I moved through the best art schools in the area. Every summer I traveled for seminars with Aunt Madge's friends at San Francisco State, and every year I went, I got better, so much better, in fact, that when I was sixteen the lab instructor, an MFA candidate at Rice University—where I was then taking advanced studio courses on a full scholarship—asked me was I for real or what?

My father told me to be kind. He said that if I wanted to leave and make something larger of myself, then I had to keep my head down and stay quiet.

"Do the work," he said. "Make the work you. Keep doing the work when everyone else stops. Don't get too sad. Don't give in to the market. Do the work even if nobody else ever notices you're doing it. Don't assume you know. Don't disrespect. Don't be loud. Don't act crass. Don't stop changing the way you speak and see and feel. Don't blow your heart with wine. Don't forget to chortle. Don't ever stop calling your mother."

When the time came, I applied to Yale, the Rochester Institute of Technology, CalArts, the Rhode Island School of Design, and Take Creek. I got in everywhere. Take Creek was my number one by a long shot.

One afternoon, my parents sat me down on the sofa. My mother hugged me and wouldn't let go. My father patted my back and smiled. He wanted me to know that he and my mother were prouder than proud of me and that he had no idea how such a talented and thoughtful boy could be the offspring of him, a poor midrange sap from Schulenburg, and her, a poor midrange sap from Magravia. He patted my back again and leaned forward, clasping his hands into a steeple above his lap. Night had fallen. Houston was heavy-hot. My mother sipped her plum wine from a bent straw. My father went on, speaking to me slowly, calmly, measuring out each word as if it were his last.

"I don't want to freak you out now, or detract from your accomplishments, but I need you to be sure this is what you want. What I mean here, son, is this tuition is a sum of money that your mother and I can't stomach, not even fractionally. So if you want to go to Take Creek, you'll have to borrow on your own, and if you borrow on your own, you need to know that this is a sum of money that can ruin your world and follow you around forever, like a curse, like a sick man. So now then, the question you need to ask yourself is this: even if you know that Take Creek will put you in the hole for hundreds of thousands of dollars, plus interest, tearing you apart for more or less the rest of your warm-blooded life on this earth, is Take Creek still what you want more than anything else?"

I said yes.

5

Char Dansdottir was six foot one, six foot eight with the hair. The hair was black with white streaks, and it popped straight up at the bangs and fell just above the shoulders. Char grew up on the coast of Oregon, outside of a small town called Port Orford. They had come to Take Creek to study fiction writing, which meant they were here for Jacobs. They were mild-mannered, always gracious in affect, and totally unassuming for a writer.

We sat drinking tea in The Den, idling, hiding away from the noise. At this hour, The Barracks sounded like a hive of buzz and activity, rife with conversations, shouts and arguments, all kinds of meaningless drivel. I poured us more tea. Char was telling me all about their latest work.

"I'm working on a new piece about a genderqueer savant trapped inside a spaceship," they said.

"Cool," I said.

"It sounds like genre," they said. "But it's not. It actually reads like a Raymond Carver story."

"Even cooler."

"The main character is a writer from Port Orford, just like me. They're picked by lottery to be shot into space with three other random people. The story is about what they see up there when they're looking down, and what happens to them while they're looking. It isn't funny, either. I'm telling you. This one's as serious as ever."

We laughed. Down the hall Jersey was yelling at Todd Mackintosh about sounding just like de Kooning again. Maria told them to shut already or else, and it seemed she had a point. Jasmine Ray Fincher, who was from Bronxville, New York, turned up the volume on her portable stereo. It was a limited pressing of Charles Mingus, live at Birdland. We all started bobbing our massive heads.

"I'm struggling with a new series on process and color," I said to Char. "I'm shooting pictures of very small objects and then repurposing them in other completely irrelevant frames."

"Sounds messy," Char said.

"It is," I said. "It's too much time at the computer, too. My eyes go slack, looking at the screen. It's hard to keep track of what I'm seeing."

"What is it that Salter always says?"

"There are so many ways of seeing. But maybe there are too many."

"He's such a fucking prophet," Char said. "And he knows it. That's what makes him such a star."

"I know. The computer just takes it all over. I love the work, but it makes me want to go out and eat a burger and a basket of fries. I get so hungry for no reason just sitting there, Char. So hungry, there's no relief."

Char put their hand on my knee. Gently, they kneaded and told me to stay light and keep breathing. They had such a knack for taking things slowly. I could never quite do the same.

"I shouldn't complain," I said. "You're a writer. You're at the computer all day too."

"I can't afford an Olivetti," Char said. "Even if I could, I don't think I could bring myself to touch it. I'm a creature of my time. What can I say? Most of the good writing I'm doing nowadays starts on my phone anyway. It's when I'm shitting, or walking, or driving, or eating breakfast. I get these spontaneous desires to write a sentence. I can do it wherever I want, as long as I'm charged."

Char paused to drink. I looked down and checked my phone. There was a message from Franny asking if I knew where she had left her purple jar of indica. I didn't respond. It was almost six now. I told Char I was getting hungry.

"I wish I were back in San Francisco," they said.

"Me, too," I said. "The lighting there. The cloudscape. That city was the closest I'll ever get."

"To what?"

"I don't know," I said. "Maybe it turned me into a monster."

"I'm not down here, but I'm not up, either. It's a strange in-between. I like it more when it gets cold. I want it to freeze and stay frozen. I want snow. I want snowdrifts. I want the plows stuck on the roads, broke down, neglected, covered in strings of bright white ice. I want not enough firewood. I want a full-on national emergency. I want something fucking crazy to happen here."

"It sounds like one of your stories," I said.

"I'm writing more right now than I have in months. I think I may have sneaked up on a novel."

"You're workshopping it."

"I wish I weren't," Char said. "Workshopping is making me a better writer, but it's also complicating my impulses. I should've stayed in San Francisco and poured beers at a bar, writing in my off time. I might have found a clearer voice there. I might have come upon my own way to do the work."

"It might've led nowhere."

"So be it. Authenticity always leads to places that most people don't understand. Most people are cowards anyway. Especially Americans. They're the worst. They act on fear. They're super stupid. Why should I follow them?"

Char was born as Charles Dansdottir. Their parents first called them Charlie. Somewhere along the way, Charlie turned to Char. The name just stuck. Char enjoyed it.

"Tell me about your name again," I said.

"Char," they said. "It's what I go by at this point in my life."

"You pulled out the letters and made it your own."

"Something like that. Making your name your own takes time and patience. I've had to experiment to find the right fit."

"Maybe your name will just keep getting shorter."

Char looked at me.

"I mean maybe one day you publish a book as Char," I said. "Then on the next book, you publish as Cha. Then on the book after that, you publish as Ch."

"And then what?" Char said. "When I die, I'll just be a flat C?"

I laughed and farted at the same time. Char spat out their tea all over the floor.

That night, walking to dinner at The Chow Hall, we passed the main parking lot by The Library. Most times the lot was empty, but today it was completely full. There were tractors and trucks and bobcats, sedans and hatchbacks and coupes. There were camper vans and buses parked next to golf carts, dirt bikes, go-carts shaped like sleds. There was a lonely-looking Harley Davidson, a matte-white lowrider covered in yellow snow. An orangeblack backhoe peaked out from under a frayed blue tarp. Two sad earth movers loomed beside it. The old Volvos, Audis, and Mercedes of our professors stretched out in finely marked rows. Salter's late-seventies Citroen wagon was parked between Franny's pickup and a mastless sailboat on a trailer. One of the tires had been slashed. Both headlights were smashed in.

Salter said expertise was possible, but it required deliberate practice.

There was a mood here that could only be rendered by the camera. Everything around me had a place.

6

THE BELL RANG. WE schlepped outside with the others, all wearing these annoyed disconsolate faces. Everyone fell silent as we formed a circle in the blueblack evening. It happened exactly the same, every Wednesday night, right before dinner. The bell would ring. We would walk to The Quad. Then Grayson would come over in some heuristic outfit and get going on one of her rants.

It was a loaded event, as always.

We didn't even have a choice.

Tonight, Grayson wore a pinstriped banker's suit, a gawdy affair for fast fashion. Her nose looked swollen. Her face was glowing scarlet from too much wine. She panned the crowd as she spoke, addressing us with a large white megaphone.

"Gadgets. Computers. Applications. Constant messaging. Updates on light tasks. Habit management. Well-being consolidation. Changes in mood or body position or water temperature. All are noted. Hybridity. Online living. Total saturation and overabundance. Capital accumulation. Raw materials. Surplus labor. Expropriation. Reproduction. Debt transfer. Debt peonage."

Grayson was from California. She had a brutal commitment to lifestyle. Everything she did seemed to whisper the name of the place. Her office was full of walnut furniture, succulents, philodendrons, earthen pottery, books about balance. She kept a sourdough starter in a mason jar by the window. She had slept with the mayor of Los Angeles back in college.

"Alienation. Retrogression. Maximized return of investment. Individual Retirement Account. Diversification. Stock portfolio. Tech heavy. Initial public offering. Overvaluation. Venture capital. Liquidity. Reflexivity. Asset management. Home equity. ETF. Index funds. Dividend growth. Financial objective. Vanguard. Vanguard. Vanguard."

She carried on like that for almost an hour. It was a ministerial kind of event. The truth of this, the evil of that. No one had a clue what was happening.

At one point, I made eye contact with Gregor Toth, a gregarious Ohioan without any hair, another one of Salter's prodigies. I was usually skeptical of Gregor, almost afraid, in a way. It was the fear I reserved for the people closest to me, the ones I knew best. He stood across the circle under an overhead lamp and was lit up like a statue in the surrounding darkness, miming a suicide by playacting with a fake piece of rope. Margot Dansk was there, too, that evening. She mimed like she was trying to save him.

We went to The Chow Hall for dinner. Franny, Jersey, and I sat at the end of a long table in the wayback.

"My head just exploded," Jersey said.

"You can't feel your face," I said. "You're having trouble breathing. It's difficult to remain standing without serious effort. These are all very common side effects of a Grayson sermon."

"The world changes," Jersey said.

"And it never changes back," I said.

Every night that week, it was breakfast for dinner. One night, waffles. The next, omelets. It was something in the air, a strange liberation, somebody's ideas just floating around in the kitchen. Tonight they put out this hotel pan of egg casserole called Supremo. It had black olives and mushrooms and cubed ham and pieces of bread. Franny said that it was much like a frittata, but different because of the bread.

"That makes it strata," she said. "The plural form of stratum. A stratum is a layer or level. It's a term in the earth sciences."

"What's good is the crème fraiche and salsa verde," Jersey said.

"That's because they're made in house by cooks who work for a living wage," Franny said. "They get paid time off and stellar health insurance. There's even a matching 401k. I bet you can't say that about Yale or RISD. Can you now, Jersey?"

He rolled his eyes and flipped Franny the bird. Maybe he had a point there, or something.

"He's clearing customs now," Franny said.

We looked at her.

"He's waiting in line with the rest of them."

"What are you talking about?" Jersey said.

"Manning Lepardeux," Franny said. "He can swim more than ten kilometers on the open sea. He went to rehab twice for watching television. I heard he set sail for Tripoli all by himself when he was only thirteen. And do you know what else? There's more. Margot told me that she heard he shoots snooker like a shark. She also said he can hold his breath in freezing cold water for more than five straight minutes."

Someone wailed on a trumpet, a few tables from where we stayed. He wore a Stooges T-shirt and had a greasy beard that touched his belly. I thought his name was Rigo, but I wasn't sure, and didn't think to ask. The crème fraiche and salsa verde swirled together on my plate. Jersey informed me that the resultant color was a combination known as mint.

I reached for my camera. I took a photograph.

We ate the rest of our strata in silence.

7

I WENT TO OFFICE hours to talk about my progress.

"You're beginning to attend to the violence, kid," Salter said. "But I need you to think a lot harder about what you want from your future. You need to feel things, sense things. I need you to tell me what the world is like. Do you want to know what I think? Let me tell you, it isn't pretty. I think the world tastes like metal. I think it smells like a burning pile of plastic."

"What about photography?"

"Stupid question. Photography isn't what you think. It's actually a very conservative form. It's not so fluid. It's a way to turn moments into brute objects that have no legs. Bad news for you, I'd say, maybe. But I need your work to get even better. I need it to explode off the page, to almost kill me. Because right now you're still stuck on yourself. You have to let all that go. Are you ready to start from scratch?"

"I don't understand."

"Speed. Acid. Psilocybin. Amphetamine. Alcohol. Benzos. Opiates. Whatever you want, just take it. There are lots of ways to get yourself going. Pick any one of them, give it a try, and then let yourself just up and ride."

"You want me to take drugs and shoot?"

"You're missing the point. I want you to leave your body. I

want you to stop thinking so much, kid. That's what I want for you. You can't think your way through a photograph. Something else has to happen."

"I'll try harder. I'll focus more closely and try to see."

"Stop talking about try. Stop talking about focus. It makes me sick to my stomach. I get these urges, kid. Do you know what I'm talking about? I get these random American urges to just break shit, to light shit on fire."

"That's like Jersey."

"Why do you keep shooting Jersey?"

"He's my friend."

"What's he doing that's so interesting?"

"He's the wildest sculptor I've ever met."

"That's the most pathetic thing. You sound like a total naïf. What kind of person are you? What kind of artist do you want to be?"

"Franny says I'm the slow kind. She tells me I'm just like Char. She thinks I'm too curious about other stuff, though, so I may not hit my stride until I'm older."

"What a theory. What a bunch of sappy deershit. Look, I need kids who can grind. Do you see the work on this wall?"

"I do. It's an explosion of images. It's the entire history of the photograph as a mechanical work of art."

"Deershit. Total deershit. That's work by people who can grind. Day after day. Year after year. Grinding through process and color and subject matter. Can you grind, kid?"

"I can."

"Tell me what you like about it already."

"I like losing myself. I like engaging in activities I don't understand. There's an unspeakable quality. That means something to me. I get the urge and just shoot."

"What's Cindy Sherman up to right now?"

"I don't know, sir."

"What's Devlin's next object of concern?"

"I don't know, sir."

"Why's Andreas Gursky back in that helicopter again?"

"I don't know, sir."

"Stop calling me sir. This isn't US Guv. This is Take Fucking Creek. Take Creek wants to get you ready for Magnum. Take Creek wants to teach you how to grind."

"Me, too. I want the same."

"Get it together, kid. Get gone. And don't come back until you have proofs worth spitting on."

8

WE MET AT THE edge of the woods. We didn't speak, high five, hug, or shake hands. We just put our heads down and sighed and started walking off into the trees. When we made it to the pond, it was almost two in the morning. Maria, Char, Jasmine, and the others were already in the water, doing laps out beyond the circulator. We put on our wetsuits and swam out to join them. It was a calm, clear, cool night, concise and full of meaning. The wind blew gently through the trees. Small waves splashed across our faces. There was a fanatical simplicity to swimming like this, in a wetsuit, way upstate, in the middle of the night, miles from any city. The water level was low. It just kept falling. Warnings had been posted all over campus about the risk of bluegreen algae in the tanks.

Peter Delacroix, a maniacal Quebecois playwright, yelled for us to swim over. He wanted us to check out his tubes.

"*Enweille,*" he said. "Let's go, and let's go now."

We each grabbed a tube and climbed up. My eyes adjusted. The tubes were all tied together, bobbing along. Everyone was black in the night. There was me, Franny, Jersey, Char, Maria, Jasmine, Todd, Peter, Antonia, and Reggie Specks. Margot and Gregor and Hanna were clustered over by the circulator, talking nonsense. Soledad and Ginger Jones floated away on their noodles. They were singing a song in German. The two of them were on a real big Fritz Lang kick back then, and it didn't stop there.

Peter said, "Wasn't this great, swimming in the moonlight with nobody knowing what we were doing?"

We laughed.

"I got these on Amazon," he went on. "It was a pack of eighteen tubes. I bought three packs. The seller was reputable. The packaging was safe and environmentally conscious. The rubber wasn't from an illegal tapping operation. I find myself very pleased with this particular product."

"I'm living for the moment," Char said.

"The water smells like someone died," said Maria, whose full name was Maria Ruiz Ortega y Martinez. She was from Guerrero, Mexico, and here for post-postmodern dance. She was just like Franny, every now and then, but Maria had more urgency.

We untied our tubes. We floated away for a while. Jersey swam over and splashed us. The others followed close behind him. We had started swimming indiscriminately, making loops around the pond. We kept letting go of the tubes and heading out, then swimming back to them. Peter called this oblonging.

"I have sebaceous skin," he said. "So when I choose a foaming facial cleanser, I want that choice to matter. My choice here has exceeded every possible expectation. The shipping was fast. The price was nominal. The container was appealing, comfortable to hold, and easy to pack and store. The cleanser was gentle on the skin with a light and nutty scent. It left me feeling rather delighted. It's Peter Delacroix approved."

We were hundreds of miles from any city, but Peter could order and get anything he wanted in as little as two days. The packages piled in the hallway that led to his bunk. He reviewed everything he ordered. He had become a certified Top Reviewer. This meant that sometimes he got stuff for free, and sometimes he even shared it with us.

"I need a vacation," Jersey said. "I need a beach. I need a bungalow. I need a wet sandy towel and a break from all this art school. They've got me reading too much. I can't feel my heart anymore."

"Shut up," Gregor said. "Stop thinking so much. Just feel it. It's like swimming, like stroking along through the chop. Just fucking feel it there in your hand, you know, the water, man, the glide. It's a headfirst walk into hard wind. Just go to The Zone, Jersey. And don't come out until the work is done."

Jasmine had swum back to shore and was playing old swing songs on her guitar. Char swam over and listened. Jersey started doing somersaults underwater. Franny and I kept looping around, talking about spliffs, her best rolls.

"Once I saw you roll a spliff with one hand," I said. "You were walking across The Quad in the middle of a windstorm."

"That never happened," she said.

"I saw it. I was there. I was stunned. I didn't have my camera. There's no evidence of the event."

"Is Jersey going to be all right?"

"He has a temper that's always getting in the way of things, but he's a goddamn manic genius," I said. "I don't know, Franny. Salter says I need to just shoot. He says maybe I should take drugs. What do you think?"

Todd swam over.

"Who's taking drugs over here?"

"No one," Franny said. "Not yet anyway."

"Maybe coke," Todd said. "Maybe molly. Maybe a couple bars of Xanax. Did anyone bring beer?"

We shrugged and floated through the darkness.

"Are you meaning to tell me we have nothing to drink out here?" Todd yelled.

Margot paddled over in perfect backstroke. She wore a Speedo swim cap with the Danish flag on it, even though she was from the outskirts of Tulsa, and her parents were, too. She patted Todd on the shoulder. He let out a breathy, wet sigh.

"The Dow fell almost a thousand points today," she said. "The Nasdaq fell, too. The Nikkei. Shanghai. Hang Seng. Deutsche Börse. London. Everything. We're looking at the beginning of a recession. There's no question about it."

Margot was taking a course on the political economy of the American body. She was always talking about big numbers and fluctuations beyond our control.

It was the year before Amazon went to one-day shipping in major urban markets, the year before Governor Reiser got elected to a third term. I was shooting a Nikon D5, a Fuji GA645W, and a Contax G2 rangefinder with interchangeable ZEISS lenses. I was twenty-two years old and everything had a weight to it, an undefined sense of purpose. It was the year before Israel occupied the Sinai, the year before the hostage situation in Aden, the same year the US invaded Venezuela and dropped satellite-guided cluster bombs and Tomahawk cruise missiles on the city of Caracas.

The concerns of process and color were to occupy me intensely over the next few weeks. I tried to focus on what was missing, how I could get better, why I was having trouble seeing clearly. Then I remembered that trying and focusing were not the point. I figured the thing to do was to sit on top of a hill and slow down, to burrow, to enhance my sense of breathing. I was shooting blades of grass with a macro lens. They looked like little ears of frozen corn.

9

IN OCTOBER WE MET Manning for the first time. He was fresh off the boat from Mallorca with this prophetic, wavy hair. It flowed in a wispy dyadic down along his pea coat, looking like a true European artist. The stories around campus were legion.

He was showing in London and Rome. He already had an agent in Paris. He could reproduce a Gerhard Richter painting in less than a day. Plus, he was the only one among us to own a Hasselblad large-format camera—and he actually went out and used it.

Franny and I were eating roast beef and mash in The Chow Hall, brooding about nothing, when Manning walked in. He wore a pair of snow boots and corduroy pants. His eyes were bloodshot and a little frenetic. He filled his tray with chow, passed through the line, and came over and asked if he could sit with us.

"You know it's not snowing yet," I said, pointing to his boots.

"That means yes," Franny said, kicking me.

"Everyone here has been so gracious," Manning said.

He sat and forked a piece of roast beef and dunked it in a pile of mash before eating it.

"It's a good place," Franny said.

"Schools like this can be cold and callous," Manning said. "Believe me, I've passed through quite a few."

"We're tough, but tender, too," I said. "It's an elite institution, after all."

"Everyone's worked really hard to get here," Franny said. "Some people get a little too proud."

"We heard your parents are ostrich farmers," I said.

"That's true," Manning said. "I was raised on a farm. My journey has been complicated and strange. Someday I'll tell you all about it."

"Is it true that you can swim ten kilometers?" Franny said. "That you can hold your breath for more than three minutes?"

"Where did you hear that?" Manning said.

"Nowhere," Franny said.

"We heard you have an agent in Paris," I said.

"Her name's Claire," Manning said. "She signed me when I was fourteen."

"How old are you now?" I said.

"Twenty-eight," Manning said.

"Then why would you ever come here?" I said.

Manning made like he was thinking as he chewed. It was an intensely serious gaze. He had piercing bluegreen eyes that almost scared me.

"There's also the question of your accent," I said. "It's a no-accent. You sound Canadian. So much about you feels Canadian."

"Major works, by major artists, in major places. That's the plan. This is what they promised me anyway, back when they invited me earlier this year."

"I don't understand," Franny said.

Manning nodded. He told us he would explain everything later in greater detail. Right now he just wanted food, though. His body was totally crashing. He ate everything off his plate. Then he rose from the table and walked off for seconds. Franny and I sat there quietly and watched him. When he came back, he carried a tray full of one of the strangest assortments of chow I had ever seen.

"Look at that medley," I said, gesturing wildly. "Why do you have so much cottage cheese? Why so many spicy pickles?"

"These are foods I like," Manning said.

Franny kicked me under the table again.

"We can't all live on roast beef and mash alone," she said.

"Your plan is to do large-scale work?" I said.

"I sure hope so," Manning said. "But I need to make sure I have access to the right materials."

"What type of materials?" I said.

"I don't know yet," Manning said. "I only know they'll be very large ones. Think largeness. Think largeation. Think bigtime largening and endless largements."

"Tell us about Mallorca," Franny said.

"The summers are hot," Manning said. "Clouds are infrequent. The sea is everywhere, bold and shining."

"That sounds perfect," Franny said, leaning forward.

"What about you?" Manning said.

"I'm a dancer," Franny said. "Before Take Creek, I danced for Paul and Vivienne at a classical prep in Bushwick. Before that, I lived with anarchists who hopped boxcars and put on shows wherever they wanted. Before that, I may or may not have spent time in Troy, Montana. Nobody can confirm it."

"I love your type," Manning said. "We should go for a hike sometime. I'd really like to get into hiking."

"That'd be nice," Franny said. "I'm in sessions with Zoe in The Shaker on most days of the week, roughly from nine until four. I can make arrangements, though. What are you thinking?"

Manning turned to me and asked me what I was into.

"I'm a photographer," I said. "My background is in documentary and street. I'm trying to branch out. I'm playing around with a series on process and color. I'm not sure where it's going."

"Good," Manning said. "Knowing where you're going is total death. You need to face the uncertainty head on and let the work disclose itself."

"Salter says more or less the same thing," I said. "He's the main reason I'm here. He's one of the most important photographers of the last thirty years. Do you really have a Hasselblad?"

"I have two," Manning said. "You can borrow them whenever you want."

"I can't wait for you to meet Jersey," I said. "He's my best friend. He throws stuff around and yells at the sky just like Jackson Pollock. The thing is, he hasn't had his entire life to drink and get mad yet. It may get really exciting for him."

Jersey showed up a little while later in his coveralls and red beret. He wasn't hungry or upset tonight. He shook Manning's hand for too long and stared at him, passing judgment but not speaking. Manning asked Jersey what he was into. Jersey cocked his head.

"I sculpt and fabricate and assemble," he said. "Mostly I'm just trying not to burn shit. I get so raging sometimes, I can't help it. Take Creek can be a crazy place."

Manning nodded. It seemed like he knew exactly what Jersey was talking about. He told a story about how when he was at the Venice Biennale last year, his installation had been taken for a joke, and how he had wanted, so badly, to tear the whole thing apart right there on the spot. I could tell Jersey was really listening then. He loved it when other people confirmed his own experiences.

"Why are you here?" Jersey said.

"They're bringing me on as a transfer but that's just a formality," Manning said. "They want me to organize a show. They want to put Take Creek on the map."

"Our own biennale?" Franny said.

"Only bigger," Manning said. "More major."

Franny squealed. Her face took on this whimsical flourish.

"I would do anything," she said. "Anything to be part of that."

"Us too," I said.

Manning pointed at Franny's spliff.

"Is there more of that?" he said.

Franny burst out laughing. She couldn't stop. She laughed so hard that her braids bounced from one side of her head to the other.

"Manning, meet Franny," I said. "She's my girlfriend for going on a year now. She has a tendency to see things. And she always has a spliff pinched between her fingers."

We went out to The Farley Gardens and sat around a broken picnic table, talking story and bantering like old friends who hadn't seen each other in years. We smoked constantly. Time slowed down. My hearing went slack. I'd never been so high before. I could sense how my head attached to my body with cables and cords and fibers and circuits. Every time we finished a spliff, every time it seemed like that was it, we were out, it was all gone, and it was time to call it, Franny dug down and grabbed another spliff from some hidden recess in her bag. She climbed on the table and howled. Manning howled with her. It was one of those rare Northern nights, a forgotten relic of summer. The evening's last light seemed to hover beyond us and cast widely as it lingered.

After that, the days started to get shorter. The wind picked up. Temperatures dropped earlier than normal. We cranked the heater at night and doled out extra wool blankets. We pulled the covers over our eyes and waited. I began to sleep less, eat less, think less. I had entered a kind of torpor. Most days, I wore a green wool hat and a black field jacket with a hood. I kept unexposed rolls of film in my right pocket, exposed rolls in my left. I was shaving once every two or three weeks, showering once every three or four days. I called my parents every Sunday night and told them I was hard at work on new assignments for Salter.

Aspersions.

Cataracts.

Renderings of forms.

The useless objects of art.

10

We walked across the entire western half of Take Creek, past
The Zone, past The Shaker, past The Barracks and the Quonset
huts full of hay, beyond the power lines, the auxiliary water tanks,
the backup diesel generators, and the beekeeper's grove, and then
along the southern border of The Farley Gardens where come
spring the bougainvillea grew like a fattened, noxious weed. We
walked across the open fields and fallow pastures to the site of the
cabin that John Morrison built in 1979, just before the Shah fell,
before the price of oil rose to thirty-five dollars a barrel, before
Jean-Michel Basquiat had his first solo show in New York and
became an icon overnight.

The cabin was the staging ground for *Andy's Army*, Morrison's lifework and masterpiece. It was a field of sculptures of Andy
Warhol, one thousand in total, life sized. They were standing in
neat rows just like the terra cotta soldiers at Xi'an. All the sculptures were of Andy Warhol, but each had its own objects, its own
face, its own purpose in the field. One Andy carried a camera and
pointed. Another wielded a hoe, tilling the soil. One Andy had a
long beard. Another wore sunglasses and held a bowling ball.

I was trying to give Manning a sense of context.

"Morrison worked as a professor at Take Creek for many
years," I said. "He chose this plot for a reason, and boy, did he

choose carefully. He was given access to unlimited funds. He had plenty of time to spare. The plot is almost two acres. That's larger than two football fields. It's organized in column formation. There are twenty ranks and fifty files. Morrison made each sculpture individually. First, he formed a wire mesh armature. Then he filled the mold with styrene. Then he reinforced it with more metal wire, filled it with concrete, and built the outer layers by hand. It took him more than sixteen years to complete the field. He died a week after he finished it."

Manning and I ventured deeper into the field, getting lost in the work, forging our way, barely talking or acknowledging one another as we moved. We might as well have been alone. It was a pure absorption of space, a means to share secrets that weren't our own. It was a radical leveling, I could tell, and Manning loved every minute of it. Watching him plow through the dead grass in his snow boots and hearing him huff along from one sculpture to the next, I could tell Manning thought *Andy's Army* was yet another ridiculous American experience.

"You can sense it," I said.

"The United States of America," he said. "It's beyond approximation."

We were getting to that point as friends where we didn't have to think before we spoke. We could just open our mouths and let it flow. Everything about our relationship made sense. That day I was coming off a five-hour session on manipulation and pattern in narrative. A guest speaker named Lonnie kept running on and off the stage in different changes of clothes, spiraling and meandering through the audience, lecturing in no less than four Semitic languages. No one had a clue what was happening. The takeaway was supposed to be a poem.

We sat in the dirt by the cabin. Manning poured cold coffee from a large mason jar into two small compostable cups. He adjusted his sunglasses and leaned forward. I wanted to hear more about what came next.

"I don't know what to say about it," Manning said. "I feel like you have to spend your entire life in this country to be able to speak to this."

"Jersey has this thing against Warhol, but he loves Andy all the same. Sometimes he comes out here alone late at night just to touch stuff and make more sense."

I took a sip of coffee. Manning drew his fingers through his hair. Everything about the way he did it—the outstretched, perfect digits, the ease, the hemmed-in, untiring style—it all reeked of self-mastery, and I wanted a piece of his art. He asked whether I was making progress on the new series. I gave off a shrug that became a mope.

"It's coming along," I said. "I'm learning to be more patient."

"Franny says you're shooting blades of grass in macro," he said.

"Right."

"She says they look like little ears of corn."

"They really do."

"Salter's like a god in your field. I met him years ago at an opening in Milan. He's absolutely crazy. There's something about him, though, something odd. He has a distinctly American presence."

"How are you finding it here?" I said. "Do you like Take Creek?"

"It is strange, but I love it. I don't know how it's gotten such a hold of me. Every morning I go out to The Barn and get lost in the pits with the animals. I've been around them my whole life. I know you know that. But I've never been so excited about them. I'm tending to them, feeding them. I'm cleaning up their mess. It's the strangest thing. Why did you come here?"

"I got into a bunch of schools," I said. "But something about Take Creek spoke to me. It's just so different. It's without analogue. There's no other college like this in the world. I had to find out. Plus, Salter was here. I'd been following his work for years. What can I say? You make a choice. Take Creek was a no-brainer."

"The quiet here is not the same as the quiet in Europe. In Europe there's a polish, there's a sheen. Most everywhere in Europe has a touch of the human. Everything here has a stench. Everything's rotting. The quiet isn't close to the same. There's a hum. It sounds like a bad song. Perhaps you know what I mean."

"Franny has a lot to say about it. She says the reason's John Cage. Last year she did a show and all the dancers wore costumes shaped like characters of the alphabet. There were six dancers. Together they made a QWERTY keyboard. Jersey and Todd were on mushrooms at sold-out seats in the orchestra. Todd said that when Franny took off her clothes, which she did at the end of the show, he felt his stomach somehow exit his body and return as a jellyfish seconds later."

Manning finished his coffee. He crushed the cup in his hand. He dug a hole in the ground with the heel of his boot, dropped the cup in the hole, covered it with dirt. The sun ripped through the clouds in flittering bands, unpredictable and everchanging. Manning lit a spliff and leaned back on his elbows.

"Franny's in a cave with Zoe," he said.

"Have you seen the most recent issue of *Sputum*?" I asked.

Manning nodded.

"She's second to more or less no one," I said. "She's pretty much on top of the world."

"I'm worried that her world isn't big enough for what she's capable of," Manning said. "Franny needs some special attention. Zoe is too disciplinary. She has a history of squashing her best understudies for years."

"Franny seems happy. She won't say it but she likes the exposure. We all do."

Manning took a long drag of the spliff and passed it to me. He sat up and squinted, looking out, seeing something there that maybe he wanted. He pointed at the tree line where Jersey was walking with a chainsaw. I took another drag and passed the spliff back to Manning. We both just sat there and watched. Jersey looked around to make sure no one saw him, and then he started the chainsaw, raised it above his head, and felled a perfectly fine oak tree to the ground.

"Yesterday I went to town and bought him a fire extinguisher and a box of borax," Manning said.

We watched Jersey walk away, disappearing.

"I think he'll appreciate the gesture," I said.

11

MARIA SAT CROSS-LEGGED ON the steps outside The Library, waiting for me in freezing rain. We went inside and walked among the books, touching their spines, running our hands along the shelves. We stopped to look at the Sol LeWitt drawing on the east wall, which was cast in a hazy glow. We found a quiet study room in the basement and Maria told me more about the recent threats.

"My uncle went missing last week," she said. "My mother and father put out a notice online. A few days later, I started getting all these messages. My aunt and uncle in LA got them, too. I went to live with them when I was ten. They raised me like their own. They used all their savings so I could take private lessons. They made it possible for me to be here. I rode the train up from southern Mexico. I crossed the desert in the middle of the night. It was the hardest part of my life, but I made it through. Many others didn't. Now they're coming after my family, calling us out, asking for money. And I'm up here, stuck in the white-ass backwoods, listening to Zoe tell me how to break form."

I asked more about the messages, what they were saying, what they wanted, how they found her.

She showed me the videos, the texts, the missed phone calls, the missed FaceTime calls. She showed me how the numbers all read: NO CALLER ID. She showed me the private messages on Facebook, Instagram, and WhatsApp. Then she showed me the messages in the Secure Message Center Inbox of her online account with Wells Fargo, how they were threatening to kill her entire family if she didn't pay, and how there was nothing she could do to stop them.

Most of us had a heavy online presence. It was impossible to avoid. I, for one, had been putting my work up on Instagram for years. It was a way to reach out, meet other artists, and connect with people that cared about what I did. Most of us posted our work wherever we could, sharing it with as many people as possible. Our professors did the same, encouraging us to incorporate new technology into our daily practice.

Last year in Maria's hometown, the cartels had threatened teachers on WhatsApp and held them for ransom for their bonuses. The schools shut down for almost a month. Teachers were afraid to go outside and the students stayed home and avoided public spaces. People in the community lit candles in their windows at night to show their support, and some of them even died for it, many of them, in fact, and there was nothing she could do to stop it.

"What can I do?" I said.

"You sound like such an American idiot," Maria said. "So arrogant and so decent, but so dangerously stupid and white. People from south of the border prop up the whole American show. What can you do? Change your way of living, perhaps. Your way of life is impossible without sweating brown bodies."

"I'm sorry," I said. "I know it's a nasty story. The violence is too much to make sense of."

"No, it's not," Maria said. "The violence is everywhere all at once. There are explanations. It's just like Grayson says. You only have to want to know."

"I'm blinded by empire."

"It's worse than that."

"Tell me more."

"Facebook has tens of thousands of employees combing

through posts every minute of every day, flagging stuff that violates its standards, and pulling down what it sees fit. You think those weasels care about folks in the crosshairs in Mexico? Not a chance. They're too busy going after Muslims. They've got people monitoring activity in Arabic, Indonesian, Persian, Urdu, Chinese, Bengali, Turkish, Punjabi, Hindi, Tamil, Somali. They refer to these as critical languages. The tech companies are just miming the state. And they're getting pretty good at it. They're going after anything Islam whatsoever, and they're watching it super closely. They won't tell you that, but it's true. They'll tell you they're encouraging free, fair discourse, that they're promoting a more open society. But what they're really doing is displacing the state. They're superseding your own government. YouTube has something called Highly Direct Smart Detection Flagging Technology. They'll flag a video from Yemen in no time, but in Mexico it's another story. A group in Sinaloa posted a video just last month. When it was finally flagged and removed, the video had almost two million views. Violence in Mexico is good for American business. Dead Mexicans make you want to buy."

"Have you thought about talking to the police?"

"The police?" Maria said, laughing. "Up here? Are you joking? Take Creek is one of the best art schools in the world, but this place is like the boonies. Have you been to Marlonsville? Have you mingled with the townsfolk? The police here might think I was at fault. They'd lock me up just for the hell of it. I don't even stand a chance."

"What about Zoe?" I said.

Maria's head rolled back, following her eyes.

"Zoe is from northern Europe," she said. "That woman still uses a Blackberry. She doesn't vote. She doesn't understand what's happening."

We left the study room and wandered up the stairs, coming out the back door by the tennis courts. The freezing rain had turned to snow, heavy-wet, sticky flakes. They fell from the sky, marked our faces, and dripped away later, like someone else's water. The lights on the courts were all still on, looking cinematic in bright yellow and green. I could swear there was a sound to the snow falling. We thought it was a louder cry, a whooshing.

In the far court, Salter played alone, returning serves from a brand-new ball machine. He wore a tank top and a tie-dyed bandana. He didn't even wave at us as we passed.

12

THERE WERE TEN IMAGES in the series depicting the heist of a video-tape. They were stills from a non-existent film that had never been completed. There was an argument, an altercation, then a chase down an escalator in a fleeting escape. Along came a helicopter with two men at its door, their guns drawn, clawing in. There was aerial scatter, views from above. A woman had been shot dead on the pavement.

The Violent Tapes of 1975 was a black-and-white photographic series by Argentine artist David Lamelas. Franny had heard about it from Manning, who was obsessed with Argentine conceptual art and had told her to think about choreographing something to bring the work to life. Franny had printed all ten images on silver gelatin. I sat watching her hang them above her bunk with metal thumbtacks.

"You have to build out the space, to study it, to live inside the idea if you really want to dance with it."

"This is such wild science," I said. "You're working off this obscure South American current. I bet you're reading the new Marxists. I bet you're thinking about the Dirty War. I bet you want to make pronouncements about the Falkland Islands."

"The Malvinas belong to Argentina," Franny said.

I took off my jacket and tossed it across the foot of the bed on her pink paisley quilt. There were other images hanging there, too, the ones she was pulling down. They were mostly of dancers, but there were also a few paintings and lithograph prints, photographs, sketches, and aphorisms, the types of keepsakes we carried around for years, without reason, just bare referents.

"Why are you done with these?" I said.

"I can't keep the same shots up there all the time," Franny said. "I want new inspiration. I want new feelings. I want them there in the morning when I wake up."

"We should go on a long drive, a getaway just us two. You need to get out more. I don't want you losing yourself."

"I'm taking a break from driving," Franny said.

"We'll stay in motels that close at seven," I said. "We'll eat at drive-through hot dog stands. We'll admire the streets at night without stoplights. Towns where the temperature flashes on the sign at the credit union, towns that get renamed every few years. I want to take off your clothes at the general store and have sex in a small libertarian town."

"Manning says I should go to Chisinau," Franny said.

"All of a sudden you want to go to Moldova? You're pulling down your old favorites, Franny. What's happening to you? Why do I feel like I'm missing something?"

"Manning says that's where everyone is converging," Franny said. "There are troupes of dancers working out of warehouses and living at the railyards in the suburbs. They're reinventing dance as we know it."

"How do you know that?"

"Trust me. It's true."

"Moldova is close to Magravia. That's where my mother is from."

"Is it really?" Franny said.

"Yes," I said. "It's not even on the map anymore."

"There's a breakaway republic nearby. I don't remember what it's called."

"You should go and check it out."

"I don't even know the name," Franny said.

"What does Zoe think about it?" I said.

"Zoe says the underground is wherever you find it."

"You're hanging out with Manning a lot."

"We're all hanging out with Manning a lot. It's good for us."

"Why am I worried?"

"I don't know," Franny said. "We're growing as people, and as artists. Manning being here is the best thing we could've ever asked for. We can connect to other worlds through him. I'm not the only one by the way. You seem to be pretty obsessed with him yourself."

"It's true," I said. "When we're together I feel like I'm changing in an immediate perceptible sense. He gives me pointers on what it is I should look for. I think it may be widening my understanding."

Franny stood up on her bunk and got face to face with one of the images. The shot in question depicted a man and woman with their backs to the camera, running to the edge of a pier. A small boat seemed to be coming to rescue them. But it wasn't clear whether they would make it.

"David Lamelas went to jail four times in the late nineteen sixties," she said. "He didn't care about the consequences. He worked outside of the box. He had a political agenda. I want an agenda now, too."

Franny kissed me and smiled. Her mouth tasted like the half-smoked spliff resting behind her ear. I grabbed her braids, flicked them around, and twirled them, one at a time, between my fingers. I told her that I loved how her mind worked and wanted to be at her side forever.

"I'll find out how to dance like that," she said. "And no one will believe what they're seeing."

It was a twenty-minute walk across campus to The Media Annex, where Salter was giving a lecture on the ontology of the lens. On the way, I stopped by The Zone to check on Jersey. He was fiddling with a new sculpture called *Total Electric Light*. It was a metal and wood tower with wire rods sticking out at scattered angles, the form of a juggler in the middle of a failed act, a piece he had been working on for years. Jersey had used fire and nails and whatever else to affix adjunct materials to the tower.

He smoked a cigarette, flicking the ash into an old paint can. His hair was disheveled and clumped into knots. He carried his little red book in his back pocket, like always. He stepped away and looked at the sculpture from a distance. He moved about the room to various points of view and talked himself down from certain eventualities. Then he got down on all fours and started baying like a dog, panting, foaming at the mouth, and cursing under his breath, just because.

I shot him with my Contax because it was all I had on me.

I shot him on two rolls of Ilford HP5 400, pushed to 1600 for low light.

It was another beautiful, random expression of his violence. He posed for me in his coveralls, holding a lighter, and listed off his reasons for not burning down the building.

13

Now, one wet Thursday evening, just after Jersey cut off all his hair and shaved his eyebrows to nothing, I hid in a closet in The Media Annex and went through a box of old photographs. There was no particular reason to go through them. It just happened. It came to pass. Then I found myself doing it. I wasn't looking for anything specific, or if I was, I didn't know where I might find it or how I might see it, if at all, in this light. It's not like I was sitting down to think through the photographs, or to make sense of them, either. I wasn't trying to get lost in them, or to be totally absorbed. I was simply sorting them, flipping through them, looking them over one by one, taxonomically, in a closet, under the lamp, moving back and forth across time. Perhaps I just was reaching for some general truth of myself, and gradually finding all the things I had lost without knowing it.

Salter said this was the tension of photography.

Salter said it was history itself.

Here was evidence, an entire box of it, that all these things, these moments, at one time truly existed. For each of us, the moment was different, but it always persisted just the same, in complete banality, indifferent, a manifestation of the ordinary. And there was no other moment quite like it; the moment unique to a particular photograph was accessible only through that photograph.

Through the photograph, I could remember the cracks in the pavement on that cul-de-sac sidewalk back in Houston.

Through the photograph, I could remember the feeling of the vinyl seat on my first bicycle.

Through the photograph, I could remember the touch of a checkered blouse as it fell across my stomach, and how the wind blew so hard out her window that it shook the door on its hinges.

The stacks of photographs were lined up in the box in random, disorganized rows. There were contact sheets, four by sixes, five by sevens, eight by tens, and four by fours. There were sketches based on work that wasn't there, last I checked. There were photographs I had painted over, color schemes I could no longer explain.

Through the photograph I could remember the smell of that tent in San Francisco, on Army Street, under the highway, beyond The Hairball, a home constructed out of aluminum cans.

Through the photograph, I could remember my father as a young man, along with my mother standing beside him, holding a plum, and both laughing.

I could remember Franny at the natural pools at Parks Falls, way back when, up at the Canadian border. I could even remember her wearing that gaudy lime belt, dancing, mid-song, belting out lyrics in the corner of the pool with a piece of spinach stuck between her two front teeth.

These days Salter got under my skin and found new ways to stay put. I kept seeing the poster of the skier behind his desk. FIND COLORADO. What did it mean? I kept smelling his coffee and hearing his voice. I would go out walking in the woods in my free time. I circled around campus, oblonging, staging shots with pieces of kindling and other scraps of wood. Out of nowhere, Salter would appear. He would tell me what was real and what was imagined.

Now, one wet Thursday evening, just after Jersey cut off all his hair and shaved his eyebrows to nothing, and Char published their first short story in a magazine called *Splishalings*, I sat on a milk crate under a lamp in the closet and went through a box of old photographs, just because.

What seemed to make sense to me in the beginning, though, was not what came to stick. What came to stick was the significance and intensity of each and every photograph. In the beginning, the photographs were bound in a lumpy pile, but the more time I spent sorting them, the more they opened up to me, with every photograph reaching back and calling to mind its predecessor. For it was true: they belonged to no one but me, and the more time I sat there sorting them, the more each photograph spoke to me, the more I was lost to its texture, and the more I remembered about my life. Although it wasn't really remembering, not exactly, as what transpired when I looked at a photograph had very little, if anything, to do with memory. It was just a proof. A trace. And all of a sudden it seemed as if the concerns of process and color had been there all along, bearing their way through my work without my even realizing it, until now, one wet Thursday evening, sitting on a milk crate under a lamp in the closet.

I walked back to The Barracks around three in the morning in a glorious daze. I began to think about my project, where I was going, and what it all meant moving forward.

These days, Gregor channeled the spirit of an avant-garde West Coaster named Walker. Walker lived in a van. She showed at a downtown gallery in San Francisco. She built speaker cabinets and covered them with photographs. The speakers played monkish, atonal sounds. Walker set up the speakers in the middle of the gallery with muted overhead lights and security guards on rotation. The images themselves were rather odd, high-contrast video stills shot in the desert, backdropped by dry, meaningless land. The object of concern was usually a small trampoline. Sometimes Walker jumped on it.

Now, the rising moon cast The Chow Hall in a resplendent, silver-toned glow. The Quad looked like a gigantic mirror. The trees that encircled it were borders to other worlds, if only I could see them.

Salter said death was the first whisper.

Salter said that even death kept grinding, too.

Tomorrow I would go back to shooting Fujichrome slides for bright color and maximum saturation. I would reposition the background so it stood out more intensely and was more than just a setting.

I needed new stills in macro.

I needed new objects, new patterns, new lines.

I closed my eyes and counted to ten in my bunk, but the feeling wouldn't go away. I had known it from the beginning. Photography wasn't possible in the dark. Without light, there was nothing.

14

Awake. The ringing of bells. The no-sound of snow. I had to focus on breathing to know where I was. There was a piercing cry down the hall, in total darkness, the empty feeling of winter. It was far too early for birds. The smell of last night's fire was still there. The wood floor creaked softly under my feet, shuffling.

Cold.

So cold.

So very, very cold.

Awake to Jersey. Or Franny. Or Char. Or Manning. Or Todd. Or Jasmine. Or Gregor. Or whomever. Somebody was always there, already fully awake. Somebody was always flushing a toilet, wiping down a basin, putting toothpaste on a brush, summoning water from an old rusted pipe. I heard the shower turn on, then turn off, then turn back on again. Someone down the hall coughed twice. It was beautiful here and glowing. A lightbulb burned out in the closet. Many of the doors were left slightly ajar.

We got eight inches of snow on the first day, eleven on the second, and fourteen on the third. When it finally stopped falling we used our shovels to carve out the year's first tunnels on the sidewalks and paths, tunnels that would likely remain until March, tunnels that meandered, that spiraled, that undulated and crossed one another according to a hidden logic, that gave form to our movements back and forth, in and out of class, coming and going from sleep. Way upstate the snow stayed white. The northern snow had a luster. Up here, if you tried to take a picture of the snow it was no longer possible to see it at all. The snow was an aberration, this coat on things, and once it was on the ground, that was it, there would be no more, and everything just collapsed into a single lumpy mass.

I walked across the room and threw a bag of popcorn to Jersey. He passed it to Franny, and Franny showed it to Manning, flipping it on its sides. Then she put the bag in the microwave, turned it on, and tapped Manning's shoulder lustily.

"This is how we do," she said. "Two and a half minutes on high. When the time between the pops reaches two seconds, you want to pull it. It has to be old-fashioned butter. Without butter, the stuff just gets stuck in your teeth and it's not worth sucking on. Without butter, it tastes like Styrofoam."

We sat on platform sofas in The Cinema, holed up, watching movies and smoking spliffs. It was late in the afternoon. There was three feet of fresh snow on the ground outside.

"We need to talk about Warhol," Manning said, all of a sudden.

"Warhola," Jersey said. "You meant to say Warhola."

"That piece with the electric chair," Manning said.

"I don't know it," I said.

"Now there's a piece of art," Manning said. "You need to make time to know that one. It sticks inside of you. I saw two of them side by side once. One was deep cobalt, the other fluorescent orange. You're not seeing the same again after that."

"Keep talking," Franny said.

"After seeing that, death is no longer real. Death becomes a knock-knock joke. If you touch your face afterward, your face will explode into millions of pieces of glass. No one can explain it."

"What no one can explain are these tables," I said. "Who's responsible for these legs?"

The tables in The Cinema were made of wavy cuts of Plexiglas.

All the legs were covered in brightly colored foam. They looked like they were from the set of a strange movie, a movie I had seen but couldn't remember.

"Tell us about the show," Franny said.

"I'm making headway," Manning said. "I'm putting together the guest list. I'll be sending out the invitation soon. The invitation will be delivered by the US Postal Service. It will be mailed with paper and stamps. It will take time. Patience is important. Biennales are like warbirds. They have to be formed. They don't materialize out of nothing. The RSVP is printed on thin paper, much like vellum. It comes with a self-addressed stamped envelope. It has two boxes. One box says, *Oui*. The other says, *Non*. You're supposed to pick one. It's an elective procedure."

"Jersey and I want to know our roles," I said.

"The show will last a full week at the end of March," Manning said. "I don't know about any roles yet."

"I could be an usher," Jersey said.

"It's not a wedding," Franny said.

"I could be a valet," Jersey said.

"We'll need to utilize the outdoor space," Manning said. "Some of the potential attendees will want largeness like me. I need to give it to them."

Manning had been carrying a stainless steel briefcase everywhere he went. It was the type one would see in a movie about the mob. Sinister dealings of true crime, one long take in a dark, wet basement. The briefcase was full of file folders, color-coded notes, and documents written in obscure non-Indo-European languages. We presumed the notes had something to do with the show, but no one could say for sure. Whenever we asked him about it, Manning would tell us that it was all going smoothly, and that everything he had ever dreamed of was manifesting in the most interesting, startling of ways.

"We'll erect a circus tent," he said. "I'll be doing large-scale metal work. Some folks will sculpt ice. It's good for the show to embrace the idea of winter as a concrete entity. Like an ice field. Or a gallery about hockey lore. I'm getting some pushback from your idol, though. He's putting me through the ringer and then some."

"Salter?" I said.

"Just hearing his name gets my head spinning," Manning said. "He's backchanneling. He wants me to fail. He's trying to fail me and destroy me for good. I'll make sure he gets hit. Don't you worry. And I'll make sure it's a painful fall, too."

"What do you have against Salter?" I said.

"He's a fascist," Manning said. "He wants me to go back to Mallorca and die on an empty beach. I know his type. He's used to getting what he wants. I have to be careful. So do you. Anything could happen with a guy like that."

Jersey twiddled his thumbs and stared off at the white wall with nothing on it. He often zeroed in on artless spaces like that, but he rarely talked about what he saw. Franny lit a spliff and coughed. She gestured at me. Then she took off her shirt and started dancing wildly on the table.

"Who would be the better photographer?" she said. "Hitler or Jesus? Take your time. Be thoughtful."

"Where is the force in that?" I said.

Char walked in carrying an open laptop. We all flashed our teeth and growled. Char pointed at the screen and took off their hat and coat. Jersey asked what they were up to. Char waved a free hand.

"The China threat isn't real," they said. "Everyone is always talking about China, but nobody has any idea what they're saying. China this. China that. It's all nonsense. It's racist jargon. I feel liberated knowing they're all lies."

"I read about a library in northern China on the beach," I said. "It's accessible only by foot."

"People are liars," Char said.

"People are stupid," Jersey said. "Fuck America. Fuck China, too. People should be talking about art. If they talked more about art, they wouldn't sound so stupid when they started talking about China. Having a feeling for talking about art helps you become a better person, especially if you're an internationalist like me and Char and Melville and all the other good souls who ever lived in this stupid country."

"Most people who talk about art are assholes," I said. "We're probably assholes, too."

"What we are," Jersey said, "is crazy. We're forfeiting the rest of our lives to be at Take Creek."

"That's not wrong," Franny said. "I'm already one twenty in the hole, and technically I'm not even a junior. I'll probably have to sell my eggs."

"Where I come from, college is more or less free," Manning said. "The clouds are infrequent. The sea is shining."

"That sounds perfect," Franny said, leaning in, reaching for the bag of popcorn.

"We'll get out of here and default on our loans," Jersey said. "Then we'll go live in rooms the size of closets in overpriced, technocratic theme parks like New York and San Francisco. Don't tell me how to think. My finger is on the pulse."

Jersey without hair and eyebrows had this newfound gross intensity. I asked him why he cut it all off. Jersey just shrugged and said it had been necessary for reasons he couldn't explain.

"Like carrying around the little red book?" I said.

"No," Jersey said. "There are other reasons for that."

Char sat down on one of the platform sofas and kicked off their boots and started talking. They were taking a writing session with Jacobs on spontaneous electronic literature, about posting flash fiction on Reddit, about speculations and VPN servers, cryptocurrency, and the future of Tor.

"I'm working on a new piece about a punk band that stops playing music," Char said. "Everyone in the band goes on to get an MBA from Wharton, and together they go on to create a wealth management company called Flow. These folks sit around the conference table on the fortieth floor, wearing leather jackets and black jeans, all covered in tattoos, with crazy hair, with patches on their bags, with anarchist zeal, smoking cigarettes and drinking cheap bourbon, talking about games. They're setting targets. They're redefining capitalism. That's what I'm thinking about."

Manning walked over and stood by the window, looking out. Franny followed him and asked what was there.

"It's him," Manning said. "He has this way of appearing wherever I am."

"How does he know you're here?" Franny said. "How did he find you?"

Manning shook his head. Jersey twiddled his thumbs and lay back on the sofa, putting his paint-stained boots on the table.

"Nothing really matters anyway," Jersey said.

Char patted his back.

"There there," they said.

I went over to the window next to Manning and Franny and looked out. There, under a tree, in a knee-length, hooded black down parka and galoshes, Salter stood and waved. He took our photograph with his old Leica. Then he walked across the parking lot and headed to The Chow Hall, disappearing behind an oversized, Kelly green compost bin, into the soft waves of newly fallen snow.

15

I WENT TO OFFICE hours to talk about my progress.

"There are so many ways of seeing, kid. But maybe there are too many. I'm under a tight watch right now. This clumpy toad from Mallorca is giving me some good shit. Plus he's got a bunch of minions. Rumor has it you're one of them."

"Manning is my friend. He's been good to all of us."

"Ouch. That hurts bad. Real bad, kid. Even from a brazen young artist like you. I don't know what to say."

"What do you have against Manning?"

"Some higher-up brought Manning over for a show. All of you think he's some wild child. Just because he has an agent. Just because he's showing in London and Rome. Christ, I think it's the most pathetic thing. His work is deershit. It looks, smells, tastes, and feels like a steaming hot pile of Rocky Mountain deershit. I've been trying to pull off that show for years. No one listens to me. No one will do the work. I need you to start shooting him. I need to know what he's up to."

"You want me to shoot him?"

"Right."

"Like tail him and shoot him?"

"Right."

"Is that legal?"

"It's risky, but not exactly legal. Anyway your work lately really sucks. It's missing some heart."

"What about the new work?"

"Meh."

"I've been excitable. I'm seeing other objects."

"No. Not really. What you're seeing is one of the many faces of emptiness. All your new shots are subhuman. I'm not tracking."

"You said to leave my body and stop thinking."

"I didn't tell you to get all worldsick and wet the bed. This stuff is just lousy. It's like your heroes took a piss in a river and you drank it, mistaking it for holy water. Bad news for you, I think, maybe. Have you ever read Spinoza?"

"No."

"Have you ever tasted bitter melon?"

"No."

"If Spinoza is right, then every photograph is essentially of the same thing, just with different attributes and qualities. I bet that makes you sad. I bet that makes it hard to sleep at night."

"I don't follow."

"We're talking this intrinsically infinite totality. We're talking God, motherfucker."

"I don't follow."

"Look, I had a wife once out in Colorado, plus a couple kids, too. Things got heavy. I bailed. I went to shoot for Magnum. I wasn't cut out for anything else but shooting anyway. Shooting and talking about shooting. Then I ended up at Take Creek. Hear me, kid. I didn't ask for this. It just fell on me. I hate this goddamn economy. I hate having an income. But I need it. And I kind of like teaching here. They pay me really well. I feel for you kids, though. You're getting your eyes gouged with this tuition. You'll never be able to do anything with your life but owe. That really sucks. Photography isn't what you think it is. I'm telling you. I need to find out what's going on. I won't stand for some renegade European halfwit fucking with my tenure. Do you copy?"

"Yes."

"Have you ever tailed anyone, kid?"

"No."

"Once you start, it gets tricky. The following changes you. It realigns your neurons or something otherwise more radical. The following never really stops, either. It just keeps worming around the room. My old grandmother, dead now, she followed everyone, and mostly in Chicagoland, too. We're talking jazz greats. Bop. Cool. Fusion. Improv. New wave. Prog. Grandma dug on all styles. She was the original hipster."

"That's how I see Manning."

"We need some paraffin for your ears. You're coming across all blotto to me. You're missing the point. Grandma followed Miles Davis, John McLaughlin, John Coltrane, Charles Mingus, Dave Brubeck, Cannonball Adderley, Lee Morgan, Ornette Coleman, Eric Dolphy. The list goes on. She was fucking crazy, kid."

"Jasmine plays a lot of those classic records in The Barracks. Sometimes I get dizzy if I focus too hard."

"Did I ever tell you about the time Grandma heard Saul Bellow give a reading in Iowa City? Did I tell you that when she was following Bellow back to Chicago she was herself followed by a manic and drunken John Cheever in a Buick with only one working headlight? She used to say that it was like being in the middle of two sentences. Like she was the main character in a book about becoming. I loved that idea. I used to tail my wife and kids back in Colorado. Sure, you bet I did. I was like some chewed-out, Rocky Mountain psycho killer. You know the one. In the medium gray sedan. Three cars back. Wearing sunglasses and a nondescript black ballcap. Killing the camera. I was the American original, kid. Let's talk about these shots. What is this anyway?"

"It's a blade of grass."

"It looks like a fucking ear of corn. Gross. I hate corn. It comes out the same as it goes in. I hate the stuff. What are you thinking?"

"I want a stark contrast. I want to reposition the background.

I want it to pop out of the frame."

"This is pathetic. Promising student with serious Magnum potential takes a real dive, despite world-class instruction and institutional support. I've never seen anything like it in my life."

"I can't believe there's another government shutdown in Washington."

"You gotta do politics better than that. You sound like my ex-mother in-law after too much Sauvignon Blanc."

"What about the following?"

"What about it?"

"Is photography just an instance of the following?"

"That's a stupid question, kid. Photography is an attack on experience. That attack may or may not include the following. The following may or may not make photography better. Bad news for you, I think, maybe. I've been trying to hammer this into your head for a while now, but you're falling off the cliff like the skier on this poster. Find Colorado. What does that mean to you?"

"I don't know. It looks kind of like an ink blot. Are you the skier? The snow? Or the cliff?"

"I need you to listen. Photography is ultimately about death. It's about what we add to it, what we ourselves already are. You think you're getting at some fact about the world when you shoot, don't you? You're wrong. You're getting at something else. Does that make you upset? Are you losing yourself?"

"Well, I—"

"I don't care, kid. Believe me, I couldn't care less. I need you shooting with heart, purpose, and all the reckless whatnots. Don't get all emo on me now. You're going to start following Manning. Do you copy?"

"Yes."

"You can think of it as another rogue assignment for your old pal Salter. I need you to switch gears. I need you to think about the sanctity of subjects. Did you hear that Rodrigo Duterte gassed almost a thousand people at a concert hall in Manila? Did you hear that there was no one there to shoot it because he's put all the real shooters in jail? That's what I'm talking about. I need you in jail by the end of the term. I want you sweating before a firing squad in Utah or some other theocratic nation state. Now shall we perchance to endeavor this crazy project or what?"

16

"Who would be the better photographer?" Franny asked again, later that week, sitting on a bench outside the co-op, eating a cookie like a stroopwafel.

"It's still not clear," I said. "I want to say Hitler."

"Hitler lacked technical knowledge. But he had a ruthless vision for the world. He convinced people to see it with him. He gave them a new reality. Christ was too coy. He was a loser. And losers don't shoot good anywhere."

Franny stood up on the bench. She performed a perfect chassé. I reached out and touched her hips. She scooted closer. Her legs were wet with snow. I could feel myself getting warmer on the slats.

"What about Moldova?" I said.

"I don't want to go to Moldova anymore," she said. "Moldova came and went."

"A passing notion."

"More like a bad idea."

"What about David Lamelas?"

"This is all because of Lamelas, don't you see that?" Franny said. "Right now, Zoe and I are working on a dance flow that's set to a song by John Zorn. It's demanding new moves from my body. Zoe is teaching me how to retrain my muscles to do stuff they're not supposed to. Some of these moves don't even have names. Zoe refuses to give them names. She says naming them would destroy their felicity. Zoe says language is a coldblooded killer."

I buried my head in the hood of my jacket and dragged on the spliff. Early that winter it was like I was always in the right frame, the right position. It didn't matter where I was. I was always hitting the spliff, bundling up and bearing it away. The color of the spliff shifted more than once.

Manning and Jersey came walking up Main Street.

"It was the stupidest," Manning said.

"It was the absolute dumbest thing I've ever seen," Jersey said.

Hanna ran behind them in a hooded green peacoat, carrying a pair of divining rods in her hands. Small icicles formed on the tips of her dreadlocks. She didn't pick at them, per usual specs.

"You're not seeing it clearly," she said, running, out of breath. "You're missing the most important part."

Jersey rolled his eyes and flipped Hanna the bird. Maybe he had a point.

It all started that morning because Hanna got to talking about tiny houses. We were chomping away on cheesy eggs and home-fries in The Chow Hall when Hanna, apropos of nothing, began drawing pictures of this tiny house in Marlonsville, sketching it on her napkin. Manning and Jersey said Hanna was just talking a bunch of Magyar again, but Hanna wasn't having it. She offered to show us the house herself, to mark it in memory, so we lit out after lunch in Franny's pickup and drove the eighteen winding miles to town in the snow. The road coming in was too dicey then. It sparkled and shimmered and was hard to follow. We were over an hour and a half getting there. We didn't see a single other car on the road. The seatbelts in the back were all frayed. We had to pull over twice to top up the coolant. Franny honked the horn at every passing deer. We drove slowly in total silence.

Marlonsville had a small market, a gas station, a post office, a school, and a co-op run by Quakers. People would drive up from New York City at harvest time for bagsful of red kale and white donut peaches, for lambsquarters, for heirloom mizuna. Up the street was an unlit theater that showed black-and-white Russian films scored by a shoegaze trio called Moniker. Watching a show there was a truly devastating experience. Most of the seats were broken slats of pine that had been sanded and painted white. Occasionally the popcorn machine caught on fire and made this high-pitched squeal. Two doors down an old pissant named Walt always lingered outside the lone town bar, smoking his cloves, talking to no one in particular. The bookstore across the street was boarded up. The dentist office was still closed. Cars rolled down Main Street at glacial speed. There was no longer a stop sign on that corner. The dead leaves of fall were raked in heaping piles and pushed up against the ice and snow.

"I love this place," Manning said. "But that was just a small trailer with a few auxiliary materials and exterior framing. Why is everyone at war with space right now? What's wrong with space? I think space is fine."

Hanna winced, waving Manning off.

"Maybe for you," she said. "But not for me. I want to live in a tiny house. I want to make tiny art and then just give it all away to the people walking by. I'm not looking to hold on to stuff."

"Having stuff isn't bad," Manning said.

"Having stuff is horrible," Hanna said. "Having stuff is like a bunch of lead weights I'm carrying around in a bag over my shoulder. It messes up my back. It aggravates my plantar fasciitis."

"Are you talking about your heels again, Hanna?" I said.

"The left one," Hanna said. "It drives me back to bed over and over again. You better take good care of your dogs. You need them for walking around. My father came here from Hungary in 1956. He barely got out. He says you have to take care of two very special things. Your back. And then your dogs. If you don't do that, you're pretty much screwed. Your life can just fall apart. It creeps into your mental life. It poisons your arguments. I can't even imagine what the hurt would do to my painting. That's another dynamic feature of tiny house living. Ergonomic seating. Ergonomic flooring. Ergonomic bedding. Ergonomic studio design. It's a meaningful solution for the delicate human body."

"I would rather buy one of these," Jersey said, pointing at the gas station down the street. "I could really work with a gas station. Plus, it's got all that fuel in the tanks underground. It's all ready to light up. I'd like to buy a large structure and just blow it up. That's what I'd like. Especially if it's in Marlonsville. If I could buy every house and blow up the whole town, I'd do it. I'd drop out of school for that alone. I'd stop sculpting to pursue a legacy project in arson. This place gives me chills. I get lightheaded. I want to blow my nose. I want a box of tissue. It's too American. There's too much vacancy, too much static. Marlonsville has lost itself, then found itself, then lost itself again. This is happening over and over every few days here, only now every time that it happens, it happens faster. It's barely even noticeable to your average Marlonsville resident."

"Should we call them Marlonsvillians?" Hanna said.

Jersey laughed.

"I like that," he said.

"Jersey can talk for hours about what we should keep opening up to," I said.

"I'm trying out new ideas," Jersey said. "I'm eager to expose myself to the general public. I want them to know what I am capable of. I need people at large to be a lot more excitable."

I looked at Hanna.

"Did you know that Jersey can now successfully light a fire with one match and only four toothpicks, and then let that fire burn wet scraps of wood on the sidewalk in a hole he shovels out of the snow?" I said.

Hanna shook her head.

"Sometimes people gather round to tell him he's crazy," I said. "Sometimes he deigns to listen."

"Jersey will have a feature in *Artforum* next year," Franny said.

"He heads to PS1 in May for a rare commission. I can't believe I used to swirl his penis in the shower back at college upstate."

"That isn't happening anymore," Jersey said. "Nowadays you're touching the penis of one of Magnum's hottest new stars. It's the wildest way you could've ever pictured your life going. Not me, though. Nothing about me is wild. I'm a monk in a cave working on a mandala. I'm avoiding erection. I'm resisting ejaculation. No touching. No sucking. No sex. No masturbation. This is focus, focus in its purest, rawest state, which is really just a form of meditation anyway, but I'm sure you guys already know that."

Hanna took the divining rods in her hands and pointed them straight out from her body like a pair of pistols. She started walking back and forth on Main Street. The four of us just sat there and watched. It was likely there were questions we could have posed to Hanna. It was likely there were relevant comments, echoes of feedback, observations, methodological constraints. Surely we could have interpreted her reasoning, but it was easier to just absorb Hanna in the act, walking around like a manic alchemist.

Was she looking for water? Ore? Gemstones? Oil? A tomb? A secret language? Some kind of void?

No one could say.

Hanna was pacing around now at a point maybe fifty yards away. When she stepped closer to the point the rods went crossed in her hands. She lay down in the snow and yelled out in Hungarian. We didn't understand.

"There she goes talking in tongues again," Jersey said. "I bet she's a closet fascist."

The co-op closed at three. It wouldn't reopen for four whole days. We smoked a second spliff at the small park across the street, and just as we were lighting a third it stopped snowing and the sun came out and the temperature dropped about ten degrees. The wind kicked up from the north. Snow started swirling in the air.

Lake effect.

Light effect.

Emulsion, properties of nature.

I walked around town for an hour or so, all alone now, taking pictures. A white-eyed woman rode by on a dozer, plowing the streets for free. A small boy made snow angels in the middle of a driveway. Smoke billowed from the chimneys, the lights went up, and the kettles were put on the stovetops for pots of tea. The wool blankets were laid over the children as they curled up by the fire with the TV roaring. They balanced their tablets and phones on their laps, watching old favorites, just because.

On the drive back to Take Creek I started shooting the first pictures of Manning for Salter. I shot him from the backseat on my Nikon D5 in a custom function called hyperglossia, which rendered this oil-bright videographic glow. At one point I nodded off, and when I woke up I was holding the camera to my chest, hugging it like a boy. Somewhere close to campus Manning winked at Franny and put his hand on her leg. I shot it. Franny winked back.

17

I WENT TO SEE Char, then Jersey, then Maria, then Franny. But no one was where they were supposed to be. Everything was missing. A silence hovered over all our familiar places and Take Creek became instantly foreign. I knew the schedules of everyone close to me. I knew Jersey took his nap between four and five. Char wrote in the morning after breakfast, went to workshop with Jacobs, and read all afternoon in The Den. Franny was in The Shaker all day every day working on her new piece with Zoe, obsessing over David Lamelas and the atonal progressions of an obscure John Zorn album recorded in the attic of the YMCA on Roosevelt Island. Maria was likely to be right there with her. But now everyone was gone. They seemed to have vanished. I couldn't find them. I was lost.

I walked back across The Quad, leaning forward into the wind. I went to The Media Annex and took the stairs down to the lab. Gregor was sitting on a couch, reading a book about how to pay better attention to the nature of the moment. I sat and asked him what he was working on.

"I had this dream of a magazine," Gregor said. "I was holding a magazine. On every page there was an image of the Bible. When I woke up, the suffering was over, the pain was gone, and at last I felt like I was free."

"How do you explain that?"

"Melatonin," Gregor said. "I've been experimenting with heavy doses. I want to induce an eight-to-ten-hour REM cycle. I want to maximize dream time."

"Tell me about your suffering," I said.

"You have to be calculated to achieve it. You have to give up smoking. You can't drink alcohol or caffeine. No more transfats or processed hypoallergenic foods. I'm not saying it has to be all organic, but all organic can't hurt."

"You mean the pain goes deep down into your body."

"That's right. It goes all the way into your insides. You have to get clean or it'll eat you from the inside out. I'm petitioning now for an exception from livestock duties in the morning. I can't be exposed to the toxins. Farm animals are reservoirs for all kinds of madness and infection. They'll surely contaminate my sleep."

"Are the new dreams peaceful?"

"They're filthy," Gregor said. "In the new dreams, I never take photographs. I don't have a camera. I don't even see in frames. In the new dreams, I want to pick up a gun and start shooting up crowds of bystanders for no reason. Like at a Walmart or a shopping mall. Just giving up and going for it. Expressing myself. Making it known that I'm here. I think this qualifies as progress. I've been taking pictures of benches lately. I am obsessed with the bench as a notion to be photographed. Look at these pictures, would you, please? I'm moving along this radical continuum."

Gregor put the book back on the shelf and reached for a folder. He spread out his recent shots across the table, fanning them into a collage.

"Every photograph is a bench," he said. "But not every bench is photographable in the same way."

"I don't follow."

"A thing is photographable if and only if it has already been photographed. If it has never been photographed, it's impossible to shoot."

"That has the circularity of a Salter move."

"Salter is lost in the waves. I think he's just excited to have a 401k. He could care less about shooting. Still, he's all we have. We have to stick with him."

"He's putting me on a weird assignment right now."

"It's Salter. Weird assignment is the only game in town. You better do what he says. You'll need letters if you want to go for the MFA. And you have to go for the MFA. The only thing more stupid than an MFA is a BFA. If you're good enough to keep going, you don't really have a choice."

"He asked me to follow Manning."

"Don't tell me that. That's the last thing you should tell me. If you're on assignment, you should keep it to yourself. The more people you tell the more people you implicate. I can't control how this goes for you."

"I can't do it. It feels wrong."

"You're a peon. You're a student at Take Creek. You need to do what he tells you to do. I'd love to see what you come up with."

"You want to see the shots?" I said.

"I want to see the shots," Gregor said.

"But you never want to see my shots."

"Show me the stupid shots already, would you?"

"These are different," I said. "Believe me."

"I think Manning is a dog anyway. I don't know how you trust him."

"He's a genius. I've always been scared of you, Gregor. You know that, right?"

"Who would be scared of me? I'm a lumpy creature."

"I think I'm just worried that you'll come out of here the better shooter and I'll have missed out on some important lesson."

"You can't let that happen," Gregor said.

"I can't?"

"You need to shoot benches. Or landscapes. Or street scenes.

Or studio portraits. Whatever you do, stop trying to reinvent the photograph. Every object you're shooting has already been shot."

"That's why you're so hard on the benches right now."

"I'm giving up on originality," Gregor said. "I'll shoot my benches for as long as it takes."

"Salter says I have my head up my ass."

"I've been having doubts about your new stuff, too. The blades of grass. The oddly textured backgrounds. I don't know. I think doing it like that just makes you look like a real fucking jerk."

I walked around campus all afternoon, traipsing for hours in the cold, counting my steps, mumbling to no one in low-pitched droning sounds. Every so often, the sun broke through the clouds in distended, dramatic swells, falling across campus in isolated flashes, like bands of someone else's light. I walked past the Quonset huts full of hay, past the power lines, the auxiliary water tanks, and the backup diesel generators, and then down the path along the northern cache of the beekeeper's grove to an installation called *Outer Anatolia.*

This was one of Take Creek's odder concoctions, a triptych of stone-formed mounds with holes on their tops. A guest artist named Sheldon Patton had done the piece about twenty years ago, and six months after its completion, she received a Genius Grant, left her home in Akron, Ohio, and disappeared to Turkey for close to a decade. Sheldon currently held the Chair of Aesthetics and Poetic Temperament at the Rochester Institute of Technology, and Salter downright hated her.

The idea here—I had been told by Manning, weeks back, drinking matcha with Jersey and Franny in The Chow Hall—was to crawl into the mounds one at a time, look up, and take in the sky as it appeared through the holes. But that wasn't all. The insides of the stones were etched. Each etching was a near-exact copy of a photograph. The photographs were of two types. One type, shot by unknown photographers, depicted scenes from the Japanese invasion of Manchuria. The other type, shot by Sheldon herself, showed the events of June 3, 1986, the day local police officers stormed and set fire to a public housing project in broad daylight at Laurel Homes, in Cincinnati, Ohio.

I crawled through one mound at a time. It was uncomfortable moving around. There were strains in my neck and my hands as I maneuvered through, flipping around to see the holes. I was on all fours now in the snow, looking at the etchings. I admired what Sheldon had done out here. There was a fanatical simplicity to art like this.

I went to The Barracks, then The Chow Hall, then The Zone, then The Shaker. I kept walking. I kept looking around the usual haunts, but no one was there. Everyone was still gone. Space remained this abstraction. Hours later, I was sitting by a window in The Media Annex, gazing out over The Quad, when Manning walked out of The Library with Jim Arnold and Fay Huff, two of the more powerful higher-ups at Take Creek, both of whom had a bad taste for Salter. Jim and Fay wore navy satin gowns. They looked like members of Parliament. Manning plowed along beside them in his usual corduroys and snow boots. I followed the three of them to The Admin at the far edge of campus, shooting them with my Nikon D5 the whole way there. These days I was shooting my Nikon D5 exclusively. I needed the clarity, the precision, the raw heft of digital. Nothing could be left to user error or the random chance of light. I hid behind a tree and shot hundreds of photographs, zooming in as they walked inside. A light went on in one of the rooms on the ground floor. A few minutes later the light turned off. The phone inside rang once, then stopped. It started snowing again. Night fell. Over by The Barracks, on The Quad, I could hear Grayson turning on her loudspeaker, adjusting her levels. She said she had something to say.

18

THE NEXT WEEK, WE learned that Take Creek had been selected the best undergraduate art school in the world. Jacobs appeared on *Good Morning America*, and Zoe was on the cover of *Time*. Salter flew to New York, then San Francisco, then Shanghai for interviews. All these random people came from France and Japan and Brazil, gallivanting around, taking our pictures, curious to get a taste of what we were doing. Sessions were put on hold. Farm duties were waived. The staff at The Chow Hall was working overtime just like the week before graduation. Everyone was running around. There was a grave urgency to every new day, even though none of us had anywhere specific to be. We were told by the higher-ups to be candid, to speak freely about our lives here.

Wednesday morning, I woke to a message under my bunk saying someone named Phil wanted to talk to me about it. After breakfast, I went to The Library where Phil was holding appointments in The Auxiliary Copy Room. He had a rarefied, clumsy air about him. His face was too tight, stretched out, and he needed sunshine badly. There was a rubyred stye leaking pus under his left eye. He wore a bowtie and nylon sport sandals with hiking socks. He sat at a large study table and chewed on a pen. We were surrounded by broken Xerox machines and piles of empty folders. I set my camera down on the table and took a seat. Phil asked me was I hungry again yet or not.

"I just ate," I said.

"He just ate. Our star student just took his breakfast and he's all good until lunch. Imagine that."

"There was a note under my bunk. I came as soon as I could."

"Wintertime I get hungry. I get ravenous. The bowls of chili. The sticks of cured venison. The canned vegetables. The pickled cabbage. I can't stop eating. I put on an easy fifteen to twenty every year. I think it's the weather. The inclination of cold is to eat. The inclination of hot is to forego. I think it's impressive what you kids are up to out here. I live in Virginia. It gets cold there, too, but not like this. We have shooters all over the Mid-Atlantic. Racing around in modified sedans and wagons. Running through parking lots and box stores. Threatening neighborhood festivals. Firing up town squares and college campuses. It's a far cry from the peace of Take Creek. It's a far cry from your art, I reckon."

It was the week before the stabbing spree in Buffalo, the week before a middle-aged white man from Encino opened fire on a crowd leaving a synagogue near Downtown Los Angeles.

Phil pointed at the door.

"You don't have to be here," he said. "You have to want to be here. You have to need to be here. It's one of those places. That's the essence of it."

"Something like that," I said.

"What are you engaged with?"

"I do photography. Even when I'm not doing photography I'm thinking about doing photography. It's the Take Creek motto."

"Have you seen all these people goading? Have you talked to them? Do you understand this new ranking? I could spell it out for you. But I think you already know. These are major times. The world out there is coming into some majorly major times."

"Extremely major."

"I was up this far north only once in my life," Phil said. "By way of Saskatoon. The beaten Canadian plain. It was traumatic. I couldn't go outside. I was fearful for my life. I resented other people. The bottle took hold and it didn't let go. This is the kind of college that changes people. I can see you changing on the other side of the table, moment to moment, breath to breath. Every second you're here you're remade as something else. Your cells multiply and reform as wholly novel, brand-new biological constructions. This trickles outward through the layers. It impresses upon your psyche. I have a degree in digital business administration from Rutgers. I should know."

Phil took a tissue and wiped the pus from under his eye. He asked me my size, then dug into a box on his left and handed me an ink-dyed, purple T-shirt. On the front, it read: WHY? On the back, there was a picture of a wooden canoe.

I thanked him.

Phil smiled and clapped his hands, grinning.

"The people want to know what it feels like," he said.

"What it feels like, Phil?"

"The award. The praise. The constant singing."

"It's the same as before," I said. "We're obsessed with our work. It's strange, all the commotion. Take Creek is deathly quiet. We're not used to this level of commotion."

"How noble," Phil said. "The terrified young artist just wants to focus on his craft and build up his stamina for the long haul. You're lucky you're removed from the fold. The spectacle. The American hive. The swarm of bodies. This is what it feels like. Are you listening? Can you hear it buzzing in your ears? This is the sound the world makes when the Dow falls two thousand points in a single hour."

"Grayson told us. Last Friday, she called an emergency meeting and yelled one word like five hundred times. Collapse."

"Lodging," Phil said. "You all sleep in a bunkhouse as I understand it. Correct?"

"The Barracks," I said. "That's where we stay. It's a communal arrangement. We take care of things together."

"You all eat together in a tennis bubble, too. Correct?"

"It's called The Chow Hall. It's a tennis bubble, but we never play tennis there."

"How novel."

"We just eat and talk about whatever we want. There are a bunch of long tables. You never know who's going to be there or what you're going to eat."

"I hope you're good. I hope you're really good. We may need you when you finish here. The world may need you, I mean. Though I don't think art can stop what's happening around us. I don't think it's strong enough."

"Salter would disagree."

"Have a nice day, son," Phil said. "Be sure to encourage your friends to come tell me their tales."

I went to The Zone to check on Jersey, who was hard at work on a new piece called *Fluvial*. I could tell he was really raging today. He held a struck match between his fingers. He was about to light a chair on fire with a can of white gas.

"Don't say a fucking thing," he said. "Just stay out of my way."

I loved coming over to The Zone and watching Jersey work. It gave me a sense of peace, just absorbing all his confusion. It connected me to some brutal force. I had watched Jersey rage everywhere, but when he was raging in The Zone, it was the most supreme thing. Unlike The Media Annex, The Zone was open and airy, given to this warm, saturated excess. On afternoons like today, the whole place was aglow in golden light, pouring through the windows and charging around the room, Jersey was always right there at the end of things: the starving young artist, present, awake.

Jersey dropped the match. The chair burst into purplewhite flames. He turned on a fan and sat down by the fire. He rocked back and forth like some fearless supplicant. He nodded to no one. His eyes went slack. He reached out to touch the flames as they curled off the metal, dancing, then quickly gone.

"I need more gas," he said.

"You always need more gas," I said.

Jersey walked to the window and sat back down, looking out. The hills beyond him rolled to the horizon, full of sugar maple, red oak, American beech, hickory. Snow covered the fields in silvergray waves. Jersey's head fell to his lap. He plugged his ears to block out what I took to be the voices.

"I need to be moving soon," he said. "I can't carry on like this."

"But you're better than all the rest of us combined."

Jersey laughed.

"Are you and I still traveling for the winter break?" he said.

"I can't believe you're even asking me."

"I have a plan. I'm modulating this idea for us. It involves something extraordinary."

"I'm wide open and available."

"Are you sure?" Jersey said.

"I'll do whatever you want," I said. "But I don't have any money."

"Don't worry about money. We're not going to Cancun. We're not going to Gulf Shores or Pensacola."

"Are we flying or driving?"

Jersey looked at me.

"Didn't you just say you don't have any money?"

"I have like zero money."

"Just be available," he said. "Don't worry about money."

Jersey took out his little red book from his back pocket. He found a pen on the floor and started writing. This was something new. Was he keeping notes in the little red book now? I leaned in and asked him what he was doing.

"I'm trying to explore ways of calming down," he said. "I think writing in the book may actually serve me some purpose now. After all, I've been carrying it around in my pocket, you know. It's been there for many years. It's always been empty, though. It was just this vacant space. I'm just getting started filling it out. I don't know. I've been writing little bits. I jot down notes that have nothing to do with my experience. Stuff about what I see. Stuff about geopolitics. Stuff about team sports. I just make it all up as it comes."

"Since when, Jersey?"

"It started last week. I was in this session over by The Matter Bin and it just took off. One minute I was thinking about Richard Serra. The next I was writing a limerick about a refurbished lounge chair that got herpes."

"Char says that sometimes it just comes to you. They say you have to be ready. You have to be willing to listen."

"I love Char with every part of my body, but that's completely ridiculous."

"I've never seen you write."

"Well, there you go."

"There's this added intensity to you when you're writing. For all I know, you're penning the next great American novel."

"Those are the words of a penniless soothsayer," Jersey said.

"The laws of a nation," I said. "The things that can and cannot be done. Jersey is like Hammurabi. He's like Moses on top of the mountain receiving broken language from God. You need a stone tablet. Paper burns. Paper gets wet. Paper tears. It turns to pulp. Paper alone won't stand the test of time. Your people will always revolt. They won't take you seriously if you use paper. You need to write it down in stone."

Jersey stood up and paced, talking to himself, circling around the room. He found a commercial grade axe lying on the table, grabbed it with both hands, and threw it at a wooden stool. He missed the stool completely. The axe crashed into the wall, then spun to rest on the floor. Jersey reached for the blowtorch tucked behind the workbench, but it was out of gas so he threw that, too. Eventually, he sat back down, shook his head, and started writing again.

"Manning says it's only a stubborn fool that refuses to give in," he said.

"Maybe that's true," I said. "But I'm afraid there's no other choice."

19

THAT MORNING, I WALKED up the stairs and out the front door into stilted rays of marigold sunlight lashing down across The Quad. I held a tripod and a camera. I wore a snow camo parka and carried a backpack full of water, snacks, extra layers. My socks needed washing. My fingernails were too long and dirty. Under a nearby tree, there was a hungry-faced man who formed a snowball and licked it like a lollipop. He wore a black jean jacket with a Bad Brains patch on the back. His wiry gray beard touched the top of his belly. I thought his name was Rigo, but I wasn't sure, and I definitely didn't think to ask. I took his picture. I lit a half-smoked spliff. Then I set out looking for Manning.

These days I was shooting him wherever I could find him, honing in on this grainy, distant aesthetic. I had given up on the blades of grass. I had given up on process and color. It was awkward at first, but the more I followed Manning, the less it seemed to matter. I wasn't sure if this was the following that Salter spoke of, or if it was just a thread that belonged to someone else. I tried not to think about it too much. I tried to just hide and shoot. Meanwhile I kept passing Salter in these high-traffic spaces, spaces where we couldn't talk, where I could do nothing but nod. I had a feeling in the wall of my stomach that I was being watched, though I wasn't sure by whom. I reviewed my work alone, late night in The

Media Annex, when everyone was asleep. I had shots of Manning meeting with Franco-Italian investors. I had shots of him in The Chow Hall, The Shaker, The Zone. There were shots of Franny and Jersey and the others. There were even a few with Jacobs. One night I shot him with Maria in Laundry with his pants in a pile at his feet. Another night I shot him as he and Zoe walked arm and arm in the beekeeper's grove. Just yesterday I followed him into The Library, placed my camera between the stacks, and shot him as he was dry-humping Jasmine Fincher in the reference section next to the foreign language dictionaries. I printed everything on silver gelatin and laid the work out on the table. I studied the shots closely. I tried to extract explanation. Maybe there was a pattern emerging, meandering through the light. But then again, maybe there was nothing. I went on shooting just the same. I kept looking for Salter. Days felt like weeks felt like more. Sessions faded. The air grew colder yet. Finals Week crept up like an unannounced visitor we had never met. Everyone was running, grinding away on their projects. We were all seeking space, writing papers, position-ing frames, printing portfolios, perfecting routines, revising drafts, changing notes, changing keys, touching on steps, adjusting our tempos, begging for forgiveness and then some. While Manning packed his bags for Europe, Grayson left for Temecula, California. Jacobs took a red-eye to Abu Dhabi. Zoe drove to northern Maine in the backseat of a box truck. Most of the higher-ups flew south to Captiva, Puerto Rico, the Carolinas, Grenada, Mustique. Salter was still around, but he kept his office door locked. I went knocking down the hall. No one ever knew why.

One day I was out by the Quonset huts full of hay, stashed behind a small power station, waiting for Manning, when I did it for the first time. There was no particular reason to do it. It just happened, it came to pass, and I found myself doing it.

I started taking self-portraits. I was waiting for Manning, smoking a spliff by the edge of the woods. Then the idea just came to me. I set up the tripod with my Contax wired to a remote shutter and began firing away. After that, I was doing it every time, such that pretty soon I was shooting myself more than I was shooting Manning or anyone else. Now when I sat down to review the work, there were two stacks of photographs: one with shots of Manning, and one with shots of me. The shots of Manning were just so-so, an assortment of journalistic scree. But the shots of me shooting Manning—these had the capacity to incite something like a low-grade panic.

I began to organize a concept for a submission to Manning's show, a series of self-portraits depicting yearning, wonder, and warm, wistful shame. The grayscale of the series was devastating, the tonality as well. There was a hint of the seventies avant-garde in the new work, a circumstantial notion, perhaps, but not to be lost on everyone. Salter wouldn't believe it was me. He would think I was faking it. I was sure. He would think I was stealing the work of some bright-eyed rising star at Magnum, that I was pulling a gag and calling it my own.

The landscape kept swelling away from me. My clothes took on the vinegary stench of stop bath. My skin was dry and flaky to the touch.

I spent the rest of the day wandering around campus, looking for Manning but never finding him. I smoked another spliff and went to the water tank, where Peter Delacroix was playing with his tubes on the ice, all by himself, yelling out to no one in French. I made my way to The Farley Gardens and found Todd Mackintosh painting a tree at his easel. I realized I hadn't seen him in months.

"You look blonder," I said.

"I've been gone," Todd said, turning to me. "I went to New Caledonia with my father. He pulled me out of class. He's on a dig there right now. He wanted me to see the scale of his operation."

"Have you lost weight?"

"More than ten kilos. Would you believe it?"

"You're using kilos now."

"The rest of the world, numbnuts. That's reason enough. You

look more or less the same to me. Should I be noticing something different about you, too? I don't really remember what you looked like before I left."

"Jersey told me that your father wears a pith helmet and that he has visions of conquering the world with his broken little axe."

"Dad's a good man. An archaeologist. He cares deeply about his subjects. He plays with shards of clay and carved rocks that he finds in hovels all over the world. He believes we can read a lot of the present in our past use of tools. It sounds right. He's just a man digging around in the woods. He smokes a long cigarette. His cask pours a racy vintage. Outside it's hot. It's humid. The air smells like rotten jackfruit. Captain Cook named New Caledonia after Scotland. That was before he was killed in Hawaii. Dad says he should've been killed much sooner, as it would've spared people around the Pacific a lot of heartache. But Dad also says if it wasn't Cook, then it would've been some other peon pirate. That's what he calls them. The peon pirates. The rooks of empire. The mass murderers at sea. Dad has this way of putting things. He doesn't care what any of it sounds like. He just stamps it out there into language, and I'm telling you, it's gold. His French is improving. He wants to learn Farsi next. Then Pashto. Then Aramaic. Not for speaking, though. Aramaic would just be for kicks."

That winter, the winter in which Todd and I stood in The Farley Gardens talking about approximately nothing, was the winter inflation in Argentina hit ninety-three percent. It was the winter we moved around slowly, taping the windows wherever we could, affecting our gestures, as the courtesy of nods, a madness that was partial but only to winter, the way we bundled up and deigned to talk about the political, always hush-hush, turning up the music, spilling drinks on the floor, burrowing in, lighting the spliff, hidden from the wind under our hoods and parka poofs.

I stepped closer to Todd.

"Should you be noticing something about me?" I said.

"I don't think so, no."

"My hair is the same. My face hasn't changed. Maybe I'm shaving less. Maybe I'm putting on weight."

"Is that snow camo?" Todd said.

"You're probably just thrown. You're jet-lagged, world-weary, and a little beaten down. You're having trouble sleeping. You're macerated by modern air travel. You're coming down with a cold. You're sniffling, too. Now you're back upstate and nothing makes sense. You're feeling the South Pacific long after the fact."

"Strangely I don't remember much from before I left. Take Creek is a blur. It's like I'm having to relearn everything. New Caledonia complicated my experience. It's not easy getting back on track."

"Which is why you're painting outside in zero-degree weather."

"Right. I'm trying to force it."

"By painting a tall, dead tree?"

"Right. I'm painting a tree, but all I see are gigantic ferns backed up against the baby blue sea. I should check out the life sciences. Take Creek is a total dump."

Late afternoon, I marched alone into the woods and shot another two hundred self-portraits in various poses and likenesses. As the sun fell behind the trees, my body was cast in an enormous bulblike shadow. Over by The Barn, I heard the animals making their soft croons and laments. The goats and sheep bleated on. The roosters sometimes still crowed. I kept shooting. I kept looking for Manning. The photographs began to take on three-dimensional shapes in my head, a form of reality ballooned to pure abstraction. It was the role I played here, acting the part of the snowbound stalker who hailed from the outskirts of Houston, Texas.

20

When I got there Franny was staring at the wall, dead-quiet on her bunk. She held a blank piece of paper in her hand and was watching a movie on her laptop. I sat at the foot of the bed. I told her to guess, right now in this pithy moment, whether I was thinking about the winter break already.

"I don't really want to leave," Franny said. "I'm on a roll. I asked for special permission. They're letting me stay to work."

"Take Creek without all our noises. I wonder what it sounds like."

"It sounds like a dying fly buzzing in your ear. That's what it sounds like. If only you'd stay."

"I told Jersey I'd be his road dog. I said I'd say yes to anything. I don't know where we're going. He says he has a loose agenda."

"Jersey couldn't make an agenda to save anyone," Franny said. "Even if some uniformed fascist walked up and put a gun to his head, he couldn't do it. An agenda is contrary to his entire disposition and project."

"I'll let you know how it goes. You're the lucky one anyway. You'll be able to get so much done. It'll be like your own little residency."

"They run a limited menu at The Chow Hall. They power down certain unnecessary features. The Library is only open one day a week. Most of the buildings are locked, boarded up, and put to sleep. I think it'll be more than enough for me."

"Who else is staying?"

"I know Jasmine and Todd will be here. Manning gets back on Boxing Day. He doesn't want to miss it. I told him we're not in Canada, we're just close to Canada. He waved his hand around like I'm the idiot.

"That's perfect," I said. "He thinks the energy of the thing is somehow going to ooze across the border."

"It'll be nice to have a friend," Franny said.

"Salter isn't seeing anyone. He refuses to talk to his students."

"He probably just needs some space. You know how he gets. Is he still following Manning? Is he still just popping up?"

"I don't know," I said. "Who would follow Manning anyway? That's the dumbest thing. Manning wouldn't hurt a fly."

Franny picked at her braids, twirling them between her fingers. She grabbed my hands and fell backwards, stretching out, pulling me down with her onto the bed. Today she wore a ribbed crimson union suit. Her skin was glossy from the goat butter she used as lotion. We lay on our stomachs with our elbows propped up. I ate canned peaches with a compostable spork. Franny lit a spliff and started the movie over from the beginning.

"This thing is crazy," she said. "There are four movies in total. It's not like a TV show, though. These are four separate feature-length movies. Certain pieces connect. Most stuff doesn't. The only way to watch it is on a Finnish video-sharing website called Slant. I mean it's the only way. You can't get it anywhere. No one can. Not even on the dark web. All we know about the director is one, she's a woman, and two, she used to be a bartender in San Francisco. You know San Francisco. You spent some time there. I was hoping you'd give me some pointers."

"It's San Francisco," I said. "Pointers are hard. Every time people point at San Francisco, San Francisco points somewhere else. It forever eludes us. It keeps changing faces. People want to hold on to it in some fixed way, but they can't. The place is running away at breakneck speed, and that's how it's always been. What's your question?"

"The director is a woman, but we have no idea where she's from or how old she is or anything. All her films are in Polish. Some people think she's Polish, but I don't. I think it's just a ruse. I know she's something else. I know she has this outrageously singular human life as far as lives go. She travels to all these places you couldn't even imagine. She learns languages then forgets them. She takes pictures then loses them. She walks down streets then never comes back. I think she's just a ruse."

"How do you know this?"

"I just do," Franny said. "It's part of me to know things."

"Are all the movies set in San Francisco?"

"Mostly, yeah, and in the movies, San Francisco is crazy. It's this horrific place, full of horrific people. But everyone loves it. Everyone's infatuated. The main character is named Zofia. She's a bartender just like the director. The first scene is a ten-minute continuous take of her walking through her neighborhood a week after an earthquake. It's just horrific. It's tough to watch. The colors, too. I don't know what equipment this woman is using, but you should check it out. Remember, everything is in Polish, subtitled. Zofia has lived in San Francisco for years. She was there when all the tech companies moved in, and she was still there when they all left and the city just rolled. She hid under a small dining table with her dog during the earthquake. Most people don't even care. It's this burning wasteland. She's telling us no one ever really cared anyway. They just wanted the money. That's the gist of her work. It's like she's pointing her finger at us and laughing. It's like we think we're doing one thing but really we're doing something else. You'll see. In the movie this gets spelled out more. But mostly it's totally mundane stuff. Like you're making dinner. Or you're planting a garden. Or you're dancing or taking pictures. For Zofia, it's like every time she does something she realizes later she's actually done something else. Could you imagine that? Dancing wouldn't compute. There would be no organized performance. You'll see what I mean. It's going to stick with you. I watched the first film last week. Since then, I've watched all the way through no less than four times."

"What's this website?" I said.

"I told you. It's called Slant. It's Finnish. Two coders built out the back end in a studio apartment in the suburbs of Helsinki. Then they put together this cute little user interface for streaming. The whole thing operates on a blockchain. It's too cool for school. This is the most radical movie streaming platform in the world. And it's the only way to watch this woman's movies."

"How did you hear about all this?"

"Manning. How else? I've been working fifteen-hour days with Zoe. I barely have time to shower. I want to know if I'm doing the right thing. But I'm getting a little worried I'm in over my head now, and these movies help me a lot. They're so horrific that they make me feel better. Do you follow this? Probably you don't. You're so talented and confident. You're so far beyond these kinds of doubts. I wonder if when I finish Take Creek I'll just start something else with my life. Maybe I'll become an architect or a civil engineer. Maybe I'll manage a small company. I don't know. It's not crazy to think about. I'm not completely crazy. I think this new piece is my best work ever. But right now, I can't see my north. Not like it matters. We're so far north already. I just want to hug you and smother you for days. My heart's slowing down. These are new sensations. I see spots and I smell sulfur. I hear echoes of voices in Polish."

I told her to relax, close her eyes, and take twenty slow, natural breaths. Franny rolled to her side and curled up into my arms. I pressed the play button. A few minutes later, we were both asleep.

21

MANNING BARGED IN JUST after breakfast and called out in Catalan across the bunks. I waved him over, pretending to know what he was saying. He carried a vintage, external-frame backpack and a dark red, hard-shell suitcase covered in stamps from European train stations. His corduroy pants were freshly ironed, pressed flat against his legs, and his hair, rather curiously, was tied up in a neat bun. Absent, too, were his snow boots, replaced by a pair of strappy leather sandals. He dropped his luggage by the door, turning back. Then he walked across the room and handed me an invitation.

"Tell your friends," he said. "Mark your calendars."

The invitation was not thin like vellum, nor did it come with a self-addressed stamped envelope, nor was it in French. It was a simple three-by-five notecard, eggwhite, unlined, and written across it in black Sharpie were the words: IT'S MY SHOW, MID-SPRING, TAKE CREEK, USA.

"You're in a hurry," I said.

"A 4 p.m. flight. Connecting through JFK. Then through Paris, Charles De Gaulle. I get to Mallorca tomorrow evening. I hope my mother slaughters a duck for my arrival dinner. I'm starved for fresh poultry."

I looked at the notecard.

"I know it's not what we discussed," he said.

"It isn't even close," I said. "Biennales don't just materialize out of nothing."

"I said something like that to you, didn't I?"

"Once or twice."

"I wouldn't worry about it. There's so much time. We have this abundance of time. Life itself. Time itself. I could go on and on, but I only have a few minutes. There's a plane to catch. There's an ocean to cross."

"Are you eager to go home?" I said.

"I'm eager to eat fresh poultry. Otherwise, no, not really. I'd rather stay here. The Americas are poisoning my blood, grabbing me by the ears. Every time I open my eyes in the morning, less of what I see makes sense. I'm okay with this."

"I'm working on a new series. It's very personal. I can't explain much right now but it's my best work in years. I think I'd like to show it."

"You better," Manning said.

Char lay two bunks down, wrapped under the covers in a kind of torpor. Some days they thought it was best to just stay like that, in hiding, like persona non grata, letting the day while away to darkness. Char sat up and called out to Manning.

"Who would be the better writer?" they asked. "The Fonze or Ginger Baker?"

"The drummer from Cream?" Manning said.

"I know it's crazy," they said.

Manning was thinking.

"This one's a doozy," Char said. "Go ahead and take your time. We're talking about fiction here. Everything is a blur. It's not clear how to proceed."

"Ginger Baker," Manning said. "Ginger Baker, far and away."

"Interesting choice," Char said. "And made so quickly, with such confidence. I'll remember that."

"Is it wrong?" Manning said.

"You have to work it out very slowly to get the right

answer. You might be rushing. Let me ask you. Do you have a credit card?"

"No," Manning said. "Why?"

"Because credit cards are how us Americans get things done," Char said plainly. "You're not officially living here, breathing here, understanding here, until you're in debt here. You need to be tongue-tied to get a proper taste. Here we celebrate the human being in shackles, tied to an obscene address in Delaware. Plus, a man like you could log serious airline miles. I'm talking umpteen miles. The real traveler, the global artist, that's someone who knows how to play with their credit card. I recently got one. My mom cosigned. It's a Southwest Airlines card. There was a sizable bonus just for signing up. I wish it were Emirates or Swiss Air, but Southwest is how I reach Portland. My mom picks me up at arrivals. We head down the coast as soon as possible. Mom hates Portland. She says it's no longer worth her time."

As he was leaving, Manning pulled me aside into The Den and said he wanted to talk. I sat down on the sofa. He stood above me, looking down.

"Why are you following me?" he said.

"What are you talking about?" I said.

"Do I look like an idiot?"

"No, of course not."

"I've never seen someone so bad at disguising himself."

"Honestly, I don't know what you're talking about," I said.

"Are you kidding?" Manning said. "I saw you a few days ago. You were wearing head-to-toe snow camo."

"What's snow camo?" I said.

"Were you going deer hunting? Were the elk coming down off the mountain?"

"I would never wear a jacket like that."

"You've been following me everywhere. Haven't you?"

I shook my head.

"Don't lie to me. I know you have. I let it slide because I thought it was funny. But now I'm starting to wonder."

"I can explain," I said. "Let's just say I'm intrigued by the idea of your photographability."

"Whatever that means, whatever you're up to, you're finished with it now. The project is dead. Besides, we're good friends. Who follows around their friend?"

"For what it's worth, when I'm following you nowadays I'm mostly just taking pictures of myself."

"The world doesn't need more self-portraits."

"What does the world need, Manning?"

"You should just stick with Jersey. His intuitions are spot on. I heard he's started writing."

"I can't make sense of it. He's been carrying around the little red book for years. Then one day, he ups and starts writing. Now he can't stop."

I walked with him out the front door and across campus to the parking lot, where a school bus was leaving soon for the regional airport, known to us as Ships. The end of the term was always like that, this ever-deepening repetition. The out-of-staters formed queues in the parking lot every day at eight, ten, and noon, loading up the buses with their chicanery, their clothes, their art supplies, their fudge snacks and bowed gifts, their preparations for the long trek home. The buses were all old and loud. They ran like undying tanks, direct from campus to check-in at Ships, bobbing side to side and spewing off-white exhaust, careening through the pines like boxes of flies. The true magic moment occurred about a mile before the bus reached Marlonsville, where it passed a barn, then a creek, then a fallen mailbox, then an old abandoned homestead, after which it immediately and inexplicably exited the dead zone and entered a blissfully fast, reliable cellular network.

I stood with him in line, waiting for the others.

"I heard Jersey writes upside down," Manning said. "He likes to write hanging from the ceiling so the blood rushes straight to his head. I heard he's working on a novel."

"Who said that? You can't write upside down."

"That's not what I heard."

"Does Char know about that?" I said. "Char will be devastated if Jersey steals their craft."

"What do you mean, *steal*?"

"Come on, Manning. You know they'd be sad."

"We all have our reasons. Each and every one of us. Just look at the history. It's full of anecdotes, the stuff people did to get by, before the shows and the grants and the fame. My favorite right now is a fabricator named Asa McGibb."

"I've never heard of her."

"Go figure. She does these large-scale approximations of violence against women, only she doesn't use wood or metal or plastic. She uses leather or skin. She brings back hides from Brazil, Turkey, Argentina, India, Italy, places like that. She makes me want to fold my head into small triangles. Before she broke out, she worked as a counselor at a hospital. A social worker became a dahlia. Did you know that when Toni Morrison was editing textbooks in Syracuse, Richard Serra was starting a furniture moving business in New York? Did you know that Serra employed Philip Glass, who at the time was working as a plumber and a taxi driver? Your country just keeps getting stranger."

"How do you know all this?" I said.

"It's not a secret." Manning shook his head. "Nobody lied to you. It's all in the public record. I think you're falling behind from when I first met you. There was a real edge to you back then, You used to shine like gloss. Now you're a little too matte for me. You're dimming down. The positive for you is that the odds of this being a phase are high. It's common to move through phases. I've been back and forth between phases I don't know how many times. It's true. You can come out of it however you want. But I don't know how you'll do."

"You're feeling really good about yourself these days, aren't you?" I said.

"I'm having something of a moment," Manning said.

"I still really like you, but now I'm scared of you."

"What would I want with you?" Manning said.

"I don't know," I said. "That's what I can't figure out."

Manning put on a pair of yellow sunglasses with rosy chromatic lenses. He dropped to his knees and took a bite of old snow, slowly moving it around in his mouth, passing it from cheek to cheek, sucking it up like a piece of candy. I took his picture saying goodbye, boarding the bus and dangling out the door, and again later, when he made a big stink of blowing kisses to those of us he would leave behind.

On the way back to The Barracks, I passed the rabbi and the chaplain. They sat at a picnic table, playing backgammon. Neither of them once looked up from their game.

22

I WENT TO OFFICE hours to talk about my progress.

"I can tell just by looking at you, kid. You're failing me bad right now, aren't you?"

"I've been having a hard time getting in to see you. Your door is always locked. You're not taking visitors. When I knock, you never answer."

"It's called grading. It's called committee work. It's called the onus of being Salter. I don't need to explain myself to you. Take Creek gets busy this time of year. I've got evaluations to write, and thousands of applications for the fall term, and only four slots to fill. Your stench is much worse than normal today. You're hiding something, and it reeks."

"Manning found out."

"Already? How half-witted are you?"

"He confronted me right before he left. He's known for a while."

"Deershit. Did you tell him about me?"

"Of course not."

"What did you tell him?"

"I said I couldn't explain."

"I need a transcription. He asked what you were doing and you said what?"

"I said it was too much to explain. I said I was intrigued by the idea of him as photographable. I don't think he bought it. He questioned me specifically about the snow camo."

"Who just said snow camo? Why am I hearing the words snow camo? Am I losing my mentals?"

"I utilized a number of disguises when I was following him. Different jackets and hats. A few pairs of fleece-lined pants. Once I even dressed up in fur."

"I can see it from here. I can smell it wafting over from your side of the room. It's the side where squares always look like squares, where they always sound like squares, and they always shoot like squares, too."

"I'm not a square."

"Oh, yes, you are. You're totally just another low-fi American lackey. You probably have soft dreams of owning a home. You probably think two kids aren't enough. You might even become a swing voter in your later years, especially when you start pinching pennies and blaming poor people for your problems. I know your ilk. There are tons of folks just like you out in Colorado, but I bet Texas takes the cake. Texas is the wildest place to shoot. It's so gross it's glowing. It's utterly itself and it doesn't give a steaming bag of deershit what anyone else thinks. In Colorado now that's shifting. In Colorado, there's the vanity, the health obsession, the fitness litmus, the token love for the outdoors. Everything's channeled through corporate entertainment and like-me-now social media. I see these young Republicans for what they are. I kill them with my mind tricks when no one's looking. Uranium. Plutonium. Deuterium. Tritium. Et cetera. Most of these folks are drunken idiots riding around on scooters. They're excited about going to breweries on their off days. The wilderness is a dying notion."

"I have a new series I'd like to share with you. I've been playing around with the following. I'm obsessed with the concept. I want to invert the thing. I think it's worth exploring. This series, it's all about me. It's about the following, sure, but it looks upstream at the follower, not at the thing being followed. Does that make sense?"

"Tell me you're not shooting self-portraits."

"I'm shooting pictures of me shooting pictures of Manning."

"That's a self-portrait! By definition. How gross can it get? Nobody gives a fuzzy lump about you."

"But these are different."

"You're burning a hole in my brain, kid. You're like the unfortunate son who's castigated by the Royals. I see you wandering around the desert in the rags of a hapless vagrant, begging for alms. Wherever you go, you're spat on by the local people. No one wants you. It makes me sad. Tell me. Your family is Romanian or some such, correct?"

"Magravian."

"Sad story there. Too sad to describe. I shot for Reuters in Magravia. Nice people. Nice food. Nice language. But a mean, mad government."

"The place isn't even on the map anymore. Mom gets angry if we say the wrong things."

"Will you be visiting your sappy family over the break?"

"Jersey and I are taking a trip. He says it involves a not-so-sturdy vehicle and wits alone. We'll be checking out a lot of work by a sculptor named Jillian Arcadia. I'm looking forward to shooting what's there."

"Maybe you should take a rest from the camera. Maybe you should try knitting or looming bracelets for your friends back at the hostel. Let's see these wretched proofs. Let's see how bad they really are."

"It's a small selection. I have more."

"What's this?"

"That's me waiting for Manning in The Farley Gardens."

"And this?"

"That's me waiting for Manning over by *Andy's Army*."

"And this?"

"That's me sitting in a chair in a field, waiting for Manning. This one's overexposed and out of focus for a reason. The next one is me outside of The Library. That one is me behind the tennis courts. In all of these shots, I'm on the move."

"Look, kid. It takes me climbing a large mountain to get bone tired, like fall-over-on-the-bed-and-actually-sleep-not-just-sweat-through-the-shakes tired. But seeing these shots I feel compelled, like I just have to give in. I want to crawl into bed and I want to stay there for days. This isn't a series. This isn't a commentary on the following. These are the makings of a sleep study for big pharma. Talk me through your process. Tell me what Manning is trying to do to me."

"I've been following him everywhere. He's becoming everyone's best friend. He's building relationships. He's charming and smart. I like him a lot. This is Manning burning a milk crate with Jersey. This is Manning painting panels for a live story for Char. This is Manning with Franny crawling through *Outer Anatolia*. This is Manning kissing Zoe. This is Manning dry-humping Jasmine in The Library. This is Manning meeting with higher-ups at The Admin and turning out most of the lights."

"Pause, kid. That's Jim Arnold and Fay Huff. What's the scuttlebutt there?"

"The phone rang once, then stopped. I was stuck outside. I can't say for sure."

"Are you aware of their investigation?"

"What investigation?"

"Never mind. In moments like this you have to break and enter. There's no choice. You have to get inside. Are you coming to any conclusions about his activities?"

"Nothing conclusive."

"Is it just another bag of isolated events to you then?"

"No."

"But you can't say why?"

"Right."

"You're not tracking. There are lines of interest that connect the otherwise mediocre shots."

"I tried to find the lines, but I don't know enough about who any of these people are. It's difficult for me to gauge their intentions."

"That's some heavyset phenomenology, kid. It's the most decent thing you've said in months. Bad news for you, though, maybe."

"I'm sorry I blew it. It wasn't what I wanted. Trust me. Everything you said last time about how the following gets under your skin and stays there, how it never goes away, how it just keeps worming around the room. I remember you saying that. And now I see why. I was pretty blah about this when you first assigned it, but the more I followed Manning the more I opened up to the idea. That's how I came upon the new series. I know you don't like it. I know you hate it. But it was exciting to see where the stalking took my process."

"Stop right there. The following isn't stalking. Let's be clear on that from the start. It's something else. I already told you this but you forgot to fucking remember. This was what Grandma pined for. She said that every following was its own world, and that within that world there were all these other possible subworlds, which was why it got so hard to choose. That's the zinger of the enterprise. How to talk back to it. Are you there?"

"Maybe you could put Gregor on it. Or another student. I don't know if I can keep going."

"Gregor? You really have lost your mentals. Gregor can barely tie his laces. He can shoot okay, sure, especially in low light. But you're the only one under my watch who could pull this thing off. You can't stop now, kid. Come on. You're just getting started."

"But how?"

"You have to figure."

"He's on to me, though."

"Then get him off you. You'll never get there with an approach like that. You need more cunning."

"That's what I was going for with the snow camo."

"Who said the word? Stop killing the camera with the words snow camo. Stop farting in my chair."

"I'm sorry."

"Look, kid. I know I'm the absolute worst at this soft power. I come off real heavy. I have a strong tendency to upset. I'm not trying to be abrasive, or to hurt folks, or to bruise egos or sensibilities. But I also see no use in not speaking frankly one hundred plus percent of my life. I'll lie in my dreams. That's my promise. In my dreams is where I sleep with all my ex-wife's friends at the same time in a meadow outside of Woodland Park. I have to lie to do it, though. It takes me every ounce of energy, in the dream space, to make myself lie. You don't strike me as a liar. I spot these kinds of traits. You really are a shooter. I know you are. You just have stop trying to be all cutesy and epigrammatic. That's a stupid wave in the arts, and as a formal principle, it won't last. Stop focusing on what everyone around you is doing right now. Look at what was done before. Light worship. Human empathy. Compassion. Direct language. Expressive subjects. No dinking around or gimmicks. Minimal trickery. You need all that in the same body. I think you might have the full run of talent, but I can't keep waiting all day for it to show up. Give me a piece of your goddamn heart, kid."

"I'm digging for it."

"Dig deeper."

"Are you going anywhere for the break, Salter?"

"Don't call me Salter."

"Sorry, sir."

"I told you. Don't call me sir, either. I'm going to Arizona. I have a major donor up in the rocks in a town called Patagonia. But that's none of your business. What matters is whether you'll keep following for me. Some students lose heart over the break. They fall back into the old patterns. Mommy and Daddy give them these sloppy hugs and tell them they're the most amazing children in the world, with the most amazing art, and the most amazing potential. I can't stand Mommy and Daddy talking it all up, hyping the cause that was never really there, the cause they don't even understand. Mommy and Daddy can suck it every way to January. Mommy and Daddy are like the plague. Which reminds me. Did I ever tell you about the time I contracted malaria and dengue fever simultaneously?"

PART TWO

THE LITTLE RED BOOK

. . .

"This is probably the best time you've had in your entire life. It's going to go down as the top Take Creek experience. You can thank me for that later. In a letter. In a monograph. Or maybe just in a simple poem about the age. For the record my name is Jersey. Spelled J-E-R-S-E-Y. I know it's odd. My parents are odd people. If you met them, which someday I hope you will, the whole thing would make sense. I was more or less raised by beavers."

Pissing on a bush, unmentionable field, near Marlonsville, approximately 3 p.m. EST.

"The car is a Mazda 323 hatchback, a five speed, rusty silver, with leather seats, and loud. It blows smoke from the exhaust and three of its four tires are already bald, which is precisely why we need these chains. The stereo is lousy but it works, so I made a few playlists for us to mull over. When I say a few, I mean four. One is for thinking. One is for saying. One is for making. One is for crying."

Pumping gas in a crop-top, cable-knit sweater, West Creek, scattered clouds, with sounds of nearby children.

"Jillian Arcadia is the most underrated artist of our time. She lives in Buffalo and her work is scattered all over up here, mostly private commissions but some public. We'll be seeing as much as we can. That means we'll drive up along the border bending around toward Lake Champlain. On the way, we'll see a piece in Potsdam and later a piece near Philo. Then we'll cross the lake, stopping to see installations in the Fallen Islands, before venturing on to the town of Ripsville, north of Vincenza. Here we'll bunk with my ex-girlfriend, Daphne, who has a total of nine roommates, and most of them have two dogs. After that, we'll traverse the mountains to a quaint hamlet called Coventry, where Arcadia completed a six-month, no-strings-attached residency to do whatever she wanted on the grounds of a property that once belonged to Robert Frost. From there, we'll head to Lebanon by way of Old Canaan and New Corinth. I know, it sounds biblical. I'm excited just like you. We'll stay two nights in Lebanon instead of the usual one, but I can't tell you why. It's a surprise. After Lebanon, we'll come to our last stop near Lake Pfeifer, the home of Arcadia's niece, who looks after a cache of her aunt's early unpublished work. This is one of those things I have to see to make sense of my own life, here and now. I've made a few phone calls, but she hasn't called me back. I'm going to keep calling. You and I, no matter what it takes, we're going to see that work. I'll break down the door with my sledge if she doesn't let us in. You think I'm joking. Go ahead. Check the trunk."

Eating waffles and bacon at unmentionable diner, Long Lake Village.

"Last year over break, I went to New York by myself. I found a room in a dark alley with a twin bed, a shared bath and a lamp without a lightbulb. The heater was broken. The carpet smelled like a wet towel left out too long on the floor. This is better. I am happy in this motel room. I could write a sonnet. I could charter a boat. Or learn to tie knots. Will you please pass me that bottle of rum, please?"

Smoking in a chair by the window, Hoot Stown Lodge, Newcom,
1 a.m. EST.

"I know you don't have much money. It's fine. Usually I don't, either. But last week I got five thousand dollars from my Uncle Terry in Nome, Alaska. There was no reason for him to give it to me, he just did it. He wrapped the cash in aluminum foil and mailed it in a manila envelope. The stamps on the envelope were crooked and stained. There was a note in red crayon that read: GET RIGHT WITH GOD. He wrote the note on a piece of newspaper, over ten years old, from a town called Soldotna. Last year, all three of Terry's dogs were poisoned to death by a methy neighbor. Uncle Terry has a serious to severe drinking problem, but Mom says he's as good a man as any."

Passing through the Ra-He-Don-Mah Wilderness Area, drinking a
Red Bull while driving, turning up the playlist titled, "Music for Making."

"I need you taking care of yourself. I need you brushing twice a day. I need you eating fruits and vegetables. I need you flossing and shaving and keeping your feet clean and dry. I need you swabbing the wax out of your ears. I need you shampooing and condition-ing every time you shower. I need you changing your socks twice a day, especially when it's snowing."

Chaining up, Carthagetown, snow falling in sheets now, almost
9 a.m. EST.

"The country is better for art. It's better for human breathing. Look at this city. Look at the way it spreads out with no purpose. It's like an explosion inside a heart that no one needed. Plus it's going through one of those phases where it's too expensive for people who care about energy. I'm one of those people. But that says nothing about poor people, man. Poor people are always just getting fucked. We need to find a small town, somewhere to work, somewhere we won't be bothered, somewhere like this. But not somewhere like Take Creek. It can't be anything like Take Creek."

Perusing various maps in The Trucker's Atlas, *in this case New York City, having stopped to pee by a tree, unmentionable, nightfall.*

"Get a read on this. It's beyond speculative. It's classic Arcadia. The inside is steel. The outer shell looks like a bunch of reeds, but it's actually balsa wood covered in layer after layer of polymer to protect it from the weather. It's much larger than I expected. And much horsier, too. I know that's just incidental, though. This piece can't be horsey. Jillian hates horses. What do you see there? Are you reading animals in the piece, too? Are you seeing nature reflected back upon you? That's fair. It took me a lot of careful reflection to get past that. Now when I look, I see pure inward movement. I see a gentle curve in spacetime. What I also see is an opportunity to be weightless. If Richard Serra is the god of weight, Jillian Arcadia is the god of mutability. That gives her a load of wild shit to work with."

Visiting Hairball *(2003), a sculpture by Jillian Arcadia in Hostdam, across from the bus stop, a nearby choir singing carols.*

"Do you know what that name is anyway? It isn't Spanish, or French, or Italian, or Greek. It could be Norse or German, but I'm not sure. The internet says probably it had to do with valor and bravery, with how we interpolated that kind of person. I bet that show falls apart on him, though. I bet it comes crashing down. I bet Manning tries to steal someone's girlfriend when he gets too drunk. Just saying."

Lying in bed at the Cranston Lodge, Christmas Day, watching reruns of Suddenly Susan, *drinking rum.*

"People say travel brings us together and binds us to a common experience. But it can do the opposite, too, and pretty easily if you're not careful. For example, sometimes you make this sound that approximates a snore, but what I've come to realize from traveling with you is that that sound is actually just you as you're getting yourself ready to talk."

Ibid.

"Christmas is for swashbucklers and swine. I am so happy in this motel room."

Ibid.

"To you and me, Philo is any other place. It's a small mark on the map. It's easy to miss. But not for Franz and Kara Jaspers. They've been up here for going on fifty years, and they're pretty good at it, too. Together with their children, they run one of the most successful dairies in the country. And seeing as they both went to Pratt in the late sixties, it's no surprise they also love postconceptual art. Though Arcadia isn't exactly a postconceptualist. She's somewhere between abstract and representational. She lives in the trembling middle. When you look at her work, it's never clear what's being hashed out, or what she's getting at. The materials are sometimes found, sometimes fabricated. The political is often present but fleeting. Arcadia doesn't carry any of the old formal allegiances, nor is she involved in any scene-specific discourse. She

lives and works in Buffalo. She doesn't teach. She doesn't adver-
tise. She used to bag groceries to make rent. She used to bus tables
at the pub. Her work is the stuff of basements, and it's totally
removed from the fold. This piece here is the perfect example.
Back in the early nineties, the Jaspers commissioned Arcadia to
build a piece on their property. They wanted full control over
the project, but they wanted it to be accessible to the public, so
they worked with architects and engineers to design the turnoff
we're standing at now, a space for Arcadia to do whatever she
wanted. Their only conditions: that the piece loosely reflected
local concerns and made use of materials readily available on the
property. So what did Arcadia do? She built this. It's a library for
a sullied world. You can visit any time of day, at any time of the
year. There are no locks. The roof is hemispheric. Arcadia milled
the oak herself. For chinking, she mixed clay, sand, and silt that she
found by the bore on the property. She's playing with the idea of
the log cabin by flipping it on its side. Be careful going in. When
you walk through the door, you have to duck. You won't believe
your eyes. Here, follow me. Watch your step. Move slowly. Come
closer. Stay next to me. Notice how the shelves line the walls
from floor to ceiling, but there are no books, only movies. All the
movies are untitled, in blank cases, out of order. There's a DVD
player over there, and a projector. Do you see the pleather chair
in the middle of the room? Go sit in it. Pick a random movie off
the shelf and give it to me, then go sit down in that chair. Every
movie here is the exact same, but each one starts at a different point
in the story. You never know what you've picked until it starts,
until you're sitting in the chair watching it. But you can be assured
that every time, no matter what movie you pick, you're watching
another version of the same movie. Jillian Arcadia made this place.
It's almost useless. It stands on its own for no one but her. Time
will tell, of course. And people will talk. They'll brood over long
boring arguments. They'll bend over backwards to connect the
piece to various movements and currents, online, in the magazines,

at the lectern. Let them bleed however they want. Arcadia is right. Life itself is unclassifiable. The gist of the thing is to float."

Visiting Residual *(1999), a permanent installation by Jillian Arcadia, three point two miles west of Philo, courtesy of the Jasper Initiative.*

"Yeah, I'm writing. Of course I'm writing. What would I possibly be doing but writing? There came a moment when I had to choose. Does Jersey proceed down the same said path? Or does Jersey break form and open himself to new possibilities? I chose to start scribbling in the little red book. That doesn't mean I no longer want to burn shit. It's just that I have to get past the raging. I make note of the things that interest me. Odd notions. Aphorisms. Hyperboles. Absurd scenes. I'm suddenly concerned about when I will die, and how. I'm listening to the words I say and wondering if I'm saying them correctly. The writing seems to fit the mandates of this concern."

Chewing on a peanut butter and jelly sandwich, no crust, exiting Champlain proper, turning up the playlist titled, "Music for Thinking."

"We use *The Trucker's Atlas* because it's dependable, because people who ride the road know the road best. When it's a question of getting around, nothing comes close. Truckers are the lifeblood of this godawful nation. Truckers fill the shelves with stuff that we're supposed to buy. And if we don't buy, well then, go on and see what happens if we don't buy. Everybody knows without trucks America stops."

Smoking in a chair by the window, Woods-o-Plenty Lodge, North Fallen Island, cold pizza for dinner, light sauce.

"The Saudis are working out the kinks on a new city called Neom. It's just rocks and sand right now, but they're saying the place is pure potential. It'll run on solar and wind. There will be food grown in the desert, extensive automation, flying cars, desalinated water, an artificial moon, robots to clean, holograms to teach, fake dinosaurs, stuff like that. They have to figure for when the oil is gone. Or for when nobody wants it anymore. That's sort of similar to what Arcadia is thinking when she says, 'There will be no real endgame without meaningful altered states.' That's from an interview in *Sputum* a few years back. She's talking about the future of human consciousness. Her time in the Fallen Islands was really important. This is where she came up with her wildest notions."

Ibid.

"You're on a woodsy little island in the middle of a lake. You're driving down a narrow two-lane road peppered with boarded-up camps and cottages. You're bobbing along. You're listing. You're steering a Mazda. You're thirsty. You're hungry. You're worried there's nowhere to eat and probably you're right. Then all of a sudden there's this, next to nothing, looming in front of you as if it were carved out of the anatomical matter of air itself. You can't help but pull over and admire it. You can't explain it but you try to anyway. You're like that. You're that type of person. You're always digging for fixed causes. Soon you decide that this is what it'd be like to come upon an old metal playground that's been shattered to pieces by weather on a beach covered in slimegreen seafoam. Nobody forgets seeing it. Not even you. Jillian Arcadia just changed your life. Again."

Leaving Parallax *(1994), a permanent installation by Jillian Arcadia, South Fallen Island, courtesy of the Fallen Islands Arts Council.*

"You keep asking me why. Why, Jersey, in all our years as friends, have you never once mentioned Jillian Arcadia? I get the force of your question, but how do I explain it to you? Photography is a nefarious enterprise. Sculpture is worse. I can't tell you everything. Otherwise we wouldn't be best friends. You know that now, don't you? I am extremely happy in this motel room."

Ibid.

"Do you see the IGA supermarket there? Look just past it, on the left. Do you see the dome? That's it, coming into view now. This one is called *Umbrella Study*. You really have to wonder, as you approach it, just what exactly it was that Arcadia was going through when she made this. Depression. A bout of vertigo. Influenza. The common cold. Whatever it was, we know the woman was sick. This is clearly the work of a very sick person."

Eating cold hot dogs in the Mazda, approaching Umbrella Study *(1993), a sculpture by Jillian Arcadia, between the IGA and the Samper Federal Credit Union, 3:37 p.m. EST, 21 degrees Fahrenheit.*

"If you add it up, this isn't a long trip, but traveling with me is slow. The next town always appears in these smoky vales. There are no real stop signs. The roads don't even have names. I'll take ten to fifteen days to do what any other reasonable person would do in three. Speaking of, I'm recently feeling this dogging in the Mazda. There's a slog under the hood. I'm beginning to worry we may have a minor problem."

Smoking in bed, The Island Ho Ha Motel, watching reruns of Family Ties.

"A couple months ago I was working on a piece. You may remember. It went by the name of *Total Electric Light.* It was quite a hazardous piece, in mixed media, exploring the form of a juggler in the midst of a failed act. Do you recall that one? I tried really hard to forget about it, but I just couldn't. I started writing the mess of it down again in a new practice. Will you please pass me that bottle of rum, please?"

Ibid.

"Smoke, that's right. But not the usual kind. This is white smoke. It signals more than a minor problem. It signals head gasket, downfall, destruction, demise. That's what the mechanic told me this morning. He said it's just a matter of time. In response, I propose we skip Ripsville and head straight to Coventry. If this trip goes to the dogs, it's going to go to the dogs in Coventry, not here, do you hear me?"

Pissing on an oak tree, unmentionable field, full of forlorn water-fowl, after breakfast, leaving the Town Garage, off the Herbert Hoover Memorial Highway.

"I feel us getting fragile out here. I feel us losing control. I feel us stranded in one of these tiny towns, in the mountains, buried in ash. We're figures in some unfinished Arcadia piece. We're talking ghosts."

Ibid.

"One time when I was maybe sixteen, seventeen, I was driving my father's truck to the dump and I came upon a grief-stricken calico cat by the on-ramp. I could tell the cat was sad. Its eyes were too low. Its ears barely moved. Its face was even slumping sideways. I put the cat in the back of the truck and drove to the dump. When

I got there, the cat was still there, still with this too-sad look on its face. Afterward I drove home, and when I got there the cat was gone. I set out looking for my father, who happened to be in the garage powder-coating a beam for some new lurid piece. I told him about what had transpired. I told him I was worried the cat left because of me, because of what I'd done, a flaw in my character. He said that maybe the cat did, or maybe the cat didn't, but regardless I should write it all down before I forgot, like a dream, he said, after which you do something to honor the scope of your experience. I spent the next four weeks in the garage with my father. We sculpted a calico cat in wire mesh and put it out in our front yard by the mailbox. My father named it *Athena*. It's still there today."

Pumping gas in a black jumpsuit, Ripsville, home of Daphne and her nine roommates.

"If I could ask Richard Serra just one question, it would be: 'Where would you like to die, sir?' I bet his face wouldn't even flinch. I bet he'd just nod and mumble. I've never met him, but I've heard he's a real pompous ass."

Passing through the unincorporated community of Bolterchester, turning up the playlist titled, "Music for Crying."

"There's no wind tonight. It's too cold for snow. You should go outside and see them. The stars are like ribald satellites floating by in caustic yellow streaks."

Smoking in a chair by the window, Piney Motor Lodge, Moffett, chewing dry ramen noodles, drinking rum.

"I am freezing in this motel room."

Ibid.

"You're always asking why. Why, Jersey, in all our years as friends, have I never once mentioned Jillian Arcadia? Well, maybe I am Jillian Arcadia, or maybe I want to be Jillian Arcadia so badly that I feel like I can't tell you about her work. There's maybe been truth to this notion. Until now. Now I need the closing wall of time. Now I need the energy of a western wildfire. I need you cleaning out your pores every night before bed. I need you exfoliating. I need you watching old Brian De Palma films with the sound off, just you, in the dark, watching. I need you touching a woman. I need you touching a man. I need you touching any human body and feeling it forever in your senses. I have to believe. When I get done at Take Creek, I'm going to Buffalo to write and sculpt. You should come with me. I'm going to burrow like Arcadia. It might take years, but I'll come to mention myself someday, only later to notice if I did it all right."

Driving while drinking a Red Bull, starting over the playlist titled, "Music for Crying," another mucky wail, the overcast sky.

"Wait a second. Let me get this straight. You're what? You're following Manning for Salter? That's wicked. Who does that sort of thing? Why does Salter care about Manning? I don't understand it. Then Manning found out too? What a turn of events. That's so wicked for you. Did Manning lose it when he found out? I bet he did. Who wouldn't? You're like the town creeper with the camera, taking pictures under the skirts of little girls. You're too close to the sport. This is a new rock bottom. This is you crashing the car. Speaking of, did you just feel that jolt? Goddamnit. What's happening? The wheel's locking up. I'm getting no response from the gas. Look out the back of the car. Look at that smoke we're trailing. Jeez. It's whiter than snow. The mechanic was right. The head gasket. Plain and simple. What a savant. What a prophet. Downfall. Destruction. Demise."

Passing The Dove Estate, in the Pink Mountains, our speed falling, the car coming to a sudden stop, ten miles shy of Coventry.

"We're lucky those truckers passed when they did. We almost froze out there. We could've died. We could've been swarmed by locusts. I feel bad leaving the Mazda on the side of the road, but someone will take it. Surely they will. I can't fix everything anyway. Plus I'm still mad about this Manning situation. I feel violated. For now we should just be thankful we made it. All I know is tomorrow we're going to The Frost House and spending the day on the lawn with Arcadia. The Mazda was just a car. It's true. All cars have to die. Arcadia's work isn't like that, especially this piece. It's called *Focal*. It's her masterpiece, immune to the passing of time. I've still got a few thousand dollars on me. Did you see The Saloon down the road by the river? We should go out for pizza and pop some tops tonight, don't you think?"

Talking while showering at The Old Town Inn, one mile from The
Frost House, Coventry, no sounds of nearby children.

"I don't think Franny has any idea how much you need her. I think your codependence is becoming a problem. I think you have to reassess a boundary if you want to get these new shots. I'm not talking about what you do in other people's eyes. I'm talking about what you do for yourself, in your own work. I've had this feeling you're harboring some odd secret. Then I come to find out I'm right. We're on the road taking in Big Art, but all you're doing is shooting down, taking pictures of the snow. Are these related abstractions in our friendship? Are they accidents? Is there something you'd like to tell me while we digest that crude approximation of pizza with our bottles of rum?"

Throwing stones, drinking on the banks of the Tale River, growing
clouds, wind picking up, portending snow.

"The old ugly poet Frost is sitting at the desk, taking his time, decanting the language. He's working at a new stanza, looking out on the trees and thinking about the US of A. Then in walks Jillian Arcadia, destroyer of worlds. She throws concrete on his poems. She casts his words in aggregate. The northern literati had no idea what they were doing when they spoke up and asked for Arcadia."

Smoking in a chair by the window, preceding too long a pause, drinking rum, approximate time unknown.

"I should've gone to RISD or Yale. I should've checked out New York or Los Angeles. Yeah, I remember saying that. Maybe I was wrong, though. Maybe I'm actually where I need to be. You're probably right. You know I don't really mean all that stuff, don't you? Your work is honing in on this dark edge. If I tell you it sucks, that's only because I'm jealous. What? You're jealous of me? Really? That's crazy. I'm curving around. I'm falling down maybe. You on the other hand, you're honing. That's admirable. How are we jealous of one another at the same time? What does that mean?"

Ibid.

"It's another beautiful day in New England. I can barely feel my heart. Get a good photo of this motel room. Jeez. It looks like Elton John stopped by and stayed. We have to get moving. We're almost there. The Frost Place closes at five. We'll be there all day. Unfortunately there's no time for breakfast today. Sorry about that. You should eat one of these to hold you over."

Dressing in the dark, proffering a flavorless rice cracker, looking for his wallet and cigarettes.

"Wait a second. What's going on? The damn gate is closed. This is insane. There must be some ignoramus we can call. I'm sure they make exceptions for people like us. I'll pay a thousand, two thousand dollars to get in there. I'll pay three thousand and we can just hitchhike back to Take Creek. I bet if we barhop around town we can find someone with a key. An out-of-work janitor. Or maybe a gardener who doesn't know any better. That seems perfectly logical to me. Come on. Let's go."

Banging the gate to The Frost House, ripping off the attached sign that read: CLOSED UNTIL MARCH FOR MUCH NEEDED REPAIRS, WE APOLOGIZE FOR ANY INCONVENIENCE.

"When I came up here for orientation, we went canoeing in the Fallen Islands. I was promised four years of artistic and intellectual intensity, and endless diversions in nature. The lesson of today is that no matter how green or white or blue this part of the country is, every last slice of it is still owned like everywhere else, enclosed by fences and accessible only to those with permission. I need to see some art, is what I'm saying. I need to get inside The Frost House. Do you know anyone in this wasteland of a town who will sell me the key to that fucking gate?"

Propositioning the bartender at The Saloon, waving a twenty-dollar bill in her face, and turning around in rage as she pointed to the door, past ten, maybe fifteen, sad and confused faces, all bright red with barley and drink.

"I can't believe these dullards. How did Arcadia survive this life? Has she some innate capacity to disassociate? We came so close. I'm sorry we couldn't get in there. It stings. Really it does. But maybe we can learn from it. I'm not sure yet, though. Still I just want to be furious and set this town to flames with white gas. I hope you know this has been the most rewarding trip I've ever taken.

Thank you for being here with me. The arguments. The conversations. The teeming abandon way upstate. I feel like whatever happens now we'll always remember the year we toured around the heart of the heart of the country in the dead of winter, back when the world was simpler and the food was just fare. We were two humble pilgrims on the road to Arcadia, running out to have a look at the leaves."

Smoking in a chair by the window, Room 104, drinking rum, tearing out pages from Gideon's Bible, *and soon gone into the cold, dark night.*

PART THREE

THE SPRING

23

The hammocks were everywhere, strewn about campus in formless abandon. They were attached to trees, buildings, stone walls and chain-link fences, to stumps and statues, to bike racks, handrails, pot hangers, wicker-framed benches. Rumor had it there were over two hundred now, with more appearing every day. Many were in places where we never even set foot, by the generator, behind the tennis courts, and along the shipping and receiving dock of The Library. No one knew who was responsible, or why they were there at all.

I hung between two towering oaks on the south side of The Chow Hall. Franny hung a few feet away in a hammock of her own, content to just bob there and dangle. It was Saturday night and snowing heavily. We could barely make out each other's faces.

I asked Franny to tell me about her residency.

"It was a major failure," she said. "I did nothing but watch movies. I didn't dance, not even once. I stayed in bed for days on end, streaming movie after movie. I ate bags of popcorn from The Commissary. I showered every three or four days."

"Without other people watching you and holding you accountable, you're just another human slouch. You can't do it alone. No one can. That's why we come to art school. Most of us are too lazy. We need the structure to get things done."

"I'm ready to get back out there," Franny said. "I can't seem to wait to find my steps. Did Jersey really get arrested in the middle of New Hampshire?"

"Yes."

"Explain," she said.

"He was extremely mad because he had planned for us to visit this sculpture at Robert Frost's house, but when we got there, the place was closed for renovation, and Jersey just couldn't settle down. We went to the store so he could get another bottle of rum, and on the way back, we stopped at a bar for a drink. We had a second, then a third, then a fourth, and then Jersey bought a gram of what he believed to be cocaine from a bearded old trucker, and it all unraveled from there. We went back to the motel. It happened quite fast. There were noise complaints. Jersey lit a small fire with a comforter right outside our door. The police showed up a little while later. It didn't end well."

"He's still there then?"

"I talked to him this morning. He'll be back in a couple days, just in time for class. He said he represented himself in court and managed to convince the judge to let him walk. It sounds impossible. But you know Jersey. He gets away with everything."

"Tell me what you're feeling right now," Franny said.

I looked at her.

"I'm freezing in this hammock," I said.

Franny laughed. She rolled to her side and lit a spliff inside her jacket. She smoked it in quick bursts, carefree, unaffected by the weather.

"We're not sitting, we're lying," she said.

"We're not lying," I said. "We're hanging."

"Manning never showed up. Boxing Day came and went. I watched five movies that day. I barely moved."

I reached over and took a drag of the spliff, then leaned back and exhaled. I took another drag and held in the smoke for long as I could.

"I caught up with Gregor at lunch," I said. "We ate milky pasta with peas and Berkshire bacon. He got a phone call from Manning on Christmas Eve. He said Manning was drunk on grappa and about to board an art boat."

"An art boat?" Franny said.

"That's right. Apparently it's a large boat. You buy a ticket. You ride around. You do art. You get on. You get off. People make it up as they go. What else would it be?"

"Can I ask you a question?"

"Sure," I said. "Ask away."

"Who is Jillian Arcadia? I read about her while you were gone. The internet is teeming with theories, irrelevant details, speculations."

"I was letting Jersey indoctrinate me. I gave him full creative control. I allowed myself to be pulled along like a dog on a leash. He talked about her constantly. He says he wants to move to Buffalo to emulate her. I never looked her up. What speculations are you talking about?"

"It's all there," Franny said. "A take on Jillian's every last quality. What she wears. What she cooks. What she drives. Where she buys groceries. Where she lives. Why she doesn't vote. Why she lives without email. How she likes her coffee. What she thinks about war. Where she goes on holiday. Why she's never taken an academic appointment. It's absolutely crazy. I could see Jersey commenting on Twitter and Reddit and wherever else. I bet he's behind the scenes fueling the controversy, using various usernames, spreading rumors."

"He's writing an experimental novel partially inspired by Chairman Mao," I said. "I was with him for over two weeks. I watched him working on it. When he writes longhand, it looks like he's carving up a cadaver."

"I wish I had more to tell you," Franny said. "To be honest, it's really embarrassing. But someone said film. Someone just walked up behind me and whispered it in my ear. Film. Watch film. Study film. Interpret film. Now I'm buried in it. Meanwhile the weather is so freakish. Why would I do anything but stay inside and watch movies? Something sinister is afoot. I'm telling you. Record wind-chill. Record snowfall. Record rain. In six months it'll be the opposite. Fires everywhere. Small cities will burn. It's like one of those Polish movies we watched. It really is. The governments are run by boardroom puppets. On the surface they adorn no logos, but they're systematically destroying the world."

"You're watching too many art films," I said. "I'm worried that it's making you gloomy."

"The culture of the image is inimical to flourishing. Terrorism has eclipsed human expression."

"Where are you coming up with this stuff?"

"Most of what I just said is from this movie, *Pile*. The main character is a prizefighter named Ren. There's a scene where Ren goes off on a rant at a truck stop in Iowa. Most of what I just said is lifted straight from that rant."

"Maybe you could do a guest sermon for Grayson some night this spring."

"Don't be cute."

"I can see it now. You're blowing the horn and putting on a power suit. You're making yourself heard."

Margot Dansk walked up out of the snow, carrying a plastic bucket and a small trowel. Her lips were chapped and purpleblue and her hands trembled as she held out the bucket.

"Take an egg," she said.

"What do you mean?" I said.

"Take an egg from the bucket," Margot said. "It's a family tradition. I walk around and offer a hard-boiled egg to each and every person I encounter. It's for good luck. You can eat it later if you want."

Franny and I each took an egg from Margot's bucket. She just stood there, gazing over us absently, saying nothing.

Char walked up, wearing a mask and snorkel. A few feet

behind them, Peter Delacroix skied over on cross-country skis in a canvas one-piece suit, like an apparition in the falling snow.

"Jacobs is turning on us," Char said. "She filed for a last-minute sabbatical. They granted it to her. That means no workshops until the fall. I'm relieved but super sad."

"I thought you didn't like to workshop," I said.

"Who said that?" Char said. "I never said that. I said it was complicating my impulses, but also making me a better writer. You've been spending too much time with Jersey. He's the worst listener I've ever met."

Peter pointed his ski poles at me and Franny stretched out in our hammocks.

"You guys look miserable," he said. "You'll be frostbitten in a matter of hours."

"This hammock is freezing," I said.

"I can't feel my toes," Franny said.

"These are my new skis," Peter said. "I've even got skins if I need to start climbing. I'll be skiing everywhere until the snow melts. Skiing is good cardio. It's low impact. Char and I couldn't see more than two feet in front of us on the way over here. Luckily Margot was walking into the wind. We followed the smell of her eggs."

Jasmine Fincher and Todd Mackintosh walked up holding hands.

"Wait a minute," Char said.

"You two?" I said.

"Are coupling?" Peter said.

Jasmine and Todd bowed and laughed. We were all soon laughing with them. Everyone started hugging, patting each other's backs, and saying how good it felt to finally be back home again.

"I really missed you guys," Todd said.

Jasmine leaned in and kissed his cheek.

"Todd, if you aren't the sweetest man in the world," she said. "When are we getting married?"

Franny lit a second spliff, then a third, then a fourth. We circled around smoking, passing the spliffs, taking our time, adjusting our eyes to the dimming light. Whenever the wind welled up, the smell of freshly baked sourdough bread wafted over from The Chow Hall. I stood up from the hammock and took another drag, inhaling deeply then holding my breath. The back of my pants and jacket were frozen stiff. My legs had fallen asleep. I shook them out, running in place next to Char and making senseless high-pitched sounds.

"You're creeping up on a novel," I said.

"I'm writing it," Char said. "It's about all of us. You're the main character, too. The pages keep pouring out. I can't believe how fast it's happening."

Peter banged his ski poles together.

"You're lucky Jacobs is gone," he said. "You might be able to get some real work done for a change. Don't get me wrong. I love Take Creek. I love it so much. But I can't focus on my scripts here. I'm too busy being Peter Delacroix. I always have to present myself. I know it's a tradeoff, and it might cost me my career, but if I could extend my stay at Take Creek to five, six, seven years, I'd do it in a heartbeat."

Maria walked up with a rope tied around her waist. Soledad and Ginger Jones followed a few steps behind her. The three of them wore matching ski goggles and plodded through the field in old wooden snowshoes.

"Zoe is giving an impromptu performance of her new work," Maria said. "She's been rehearsing it over the break in Maine, and she's finally ready to share with us."

Franny sprung from her hammock, dropping the spliff in the snow and almost falling over.

"We have to go right this second," she said. "Is everyone ready? Are we missing anyone?"

"I think that's all of us," Margot said.

"I think so, too," Jasmine said.

"We can't be late," Franny said. "Zoe hates it when we're late."

It was a cold, slow walk across campus to The Shaker, and we did it single file the whole way there, following Maria but never seeing her, clenching our hands to the frozen rope. We queued up and waited outside the back entrance for almost two hours, only to be turned away at the door.

"Full house," someone said.

Franny sat down in the snow and started to cry.

24

I MADE IT TO the end of another three-hour session on Anach-
ronism and Exercise. I went for a long, hot shower, and when
I finished getting dressed, I walked to The Rec Center to meet
Jersey. He was wearing nothing but a jockstrap and a red bandanna,
climbing around in the renovated bouldering cave.

"I need to speak with you," he said, plopping on the mat.
"There's some information I need to relay to you."

"Do tell."

He gestured me for me to sit with him.

"My father might not be an artist or a carpenter," he said.

"My father might not own a roadside BBQ joint. I don't care,
Jersey. It's okay."

He closed his eyes, straining to talk.

"They took me to jail," Jersey said. "I was locked up for just
shy of six hours. Then my dad flew to the closest airport on a
Learjet and arranged for my immediate release. He's the Attorney
General for the State of New Jersey."

"It's okay, Jersey."

"Nothing about it is okay. I'm a phony and a liar. I've been
pretending to be someone I'm not."

"It seems to me we're all doing that. It's the Take Creek way."

"I'm not like you," he said. "We took vacations in the

Maldives when I was a kid. I rode a camel across a stretch of the Empty Quarter with my dad and a group of hedge fund managers. I sound like a total ass right now."

He paused and pursed his lips. The bouldering cave was quiet, and the mats we sat on were still sticky and new. I told him to keep writing, sculpting, whatever.

"Just keep making stuff," I said.

"We flew to Newark a few hours later. My dad refused to talk to me until we got home. My mom gave me a big hug and a new sweater. And these shoes were my Christmas gift."

"You've never spoken about rock climbing," I said. "Is there some hidden message in your mom giving you climbing shoes and a chalk bag?"

"She's my mom. There's always a hidden message."

"She wants you ascending. She wants you to top out already."

"Actually she just wants me to graduate and move closer to home. I told her I'm going to Buffalo. She says Buffalo is full of working-class swine. She says things like that when no one else is around."

"Can I ask you something?" I said.

"The outfit. You want to know about the outfit."

"I'm all for you wearing whatever you want, but why the jockstrap and bandanna?"

"These are from my dad," Jersey said. "He told me they complete the set."

We went out looking for Franny. We couldn't find her, though, so we just kept walking aimlessly around campus. Everyone was running, playing their part, but there was an odd energy to the landscape, and I was struggling to figure out why. The trees seemed to sag, as if tired of all the snow. The sky felt close that day, hemming us in deeper to the drabness of Jersey's mood. Later we found ourselves sitting on our haunches in The Library, looking at the Sol LeWitt drawing on the eastern wall.

"This one is called *Apogee*," I said. "I come here once or twice a week to see it. The angles never make sense to me."

"They're not supposed to," Jersey said, and laughed. "This drawing is the end of sense and the beginning of something else. Have you processed any of your shots from our Arcadia pilgrimage?"

"I think I caught some magic out there. A few of the proofs are scary good. I'm moving deathward."

"Dusty death," he said. "Describe one of the shots."

"I do them, Jersey. I don't really know how to describe them."

"Spoken like a true Take Creek original."

"Since getting back, I've had this sudden urge to travel. I think it was our trip."

"You should hitchhike," Jersey said. "You should sell all your stuff except for your cameras and a backpack."

"I don't really have much besides cameras and a backpack," I said.

"Then you have everything you need. The roaming photojournalist. The traveler. The seeker of new horizons. Salter wouldn't be opposed."

"Salter isn't back yet. I guess he's still in Arizona but there's no way to know. He won't respond to my emails."

"And all that nonsense about following Manning?"

"I have to do what he says. I guarantee you he hasn't forgotten about it. There was talk of surveillance cameras. These aren't moral commitments, you know. They're assignments. I have to complete them."

"You don't have to do anything," Jersey said. "Except die. Someday you will have to do that."

I looked up at the drawing and winced. *Apogee*, too, had an air of death to it that day, its prismatic steely lines appearing like upended mathematical truths. Sitting there on the floor, I thought we were having a meaningful experience of art. But clearly Jersey felt otherwise. He stood and threw his chalk bag at the drawing. White dust went everywhere, exploding onto the wall in a small cloud. Jersey walked over and picked up the bag. Then he flipped the drawing the bird.

25

THE CAMERAS ARRIVED ON Tuesday afternoon in a large box containing twenty-five small boxes. The residual pile of packing peanuts poured out like ice cubes onto the crooked wooden floor. The box had been postmarked in Patagonia, Arizona, by a sender named Bartleby Hanes. The note inside read:

Dear Kid,

I could get used to the desert. It reminds you about the bare essentials. It gets me to thinking about why I started shooting in the first place, which is good to remember from time to time. I came upon these cameras via a friend. I think they're perfect for your assignment. I need you to keep following for me. I need to know why that clumpy toad Manning believes he has the right to smell my shit.

The other day I was having dinner with a writer-friend named Jim. We ate coq au vin, drank French wine, and found ourselves talking about sculpture. Jim told me that Jillian Arcadia is going to be the next David Hockney, but no one knows it yet. "What gives?" I asked. "No one will care about the work in thirty years." Jim just waved me off. He's a helluva poet. A helluva novelist, too. He can write a novella

*to save your life at the brink, and he has a depth of feeling that
I can't even begin to describe. He moves at a different speed,
kid, like he knows what's worth waiting for and what's worth
letting go. At any rate, maybe he's right. You should keep
playing out the notions. Sometimes all they need are subtler
hands.*

*You better have mentionable proofs the next time we meet. I
mean that in all seriousness. You have to work harder than
everyone else. It's that simple. Most of them will give up.
Trust me. They will. Outlast them. Fly past them.*

*For now I need you to take these cameras, install them, and
watch them. Tell me what you see. I'll be back when I damn
well feel like it.*

Yours,
Salter

The cameras were round, white, military-grade, the size of an
average coaster. They looked like smoke alarms with slatted fronts
and delivered stunningly clear HD1080P video. Each camera was
outfitted with a motion detector, an infrared sensor, a six-month
battery, and a wireless transmitter that connected to Take Creek's
secure network and uploaded all video content to a website called
POMS.

Salter had included a list of locations for the cameras to be
installed. These were dubbed Nodes. Node One was in The
Barracks. Nodes Two and Three were in Manning's private
studio. Node Three was in Zoe's office. And so on. There was
a lock-picking tool taped to one of the boxes, and alongside it
a flash drive. The flash drive contained a video tutorial, roughly
fifteen minutes long, in which Salter presented a particular type
of lock and then demonstrated how to pick it with the tool. In

total he went over ten types of lock, though he said the locks at Take Creek were primarily of three types, all quite conventional, and that if I followed his instructions I wouldn't have trouble getting in. I installed all twenty-five cameras later that night when everyone was asleep.

The doors seemed to open themselves to me then. I didn't encounter a single glitch in the system.

I logged on to POMS from my phone just before I walked back to The Barracks and went to bed. The Nodes went live around five in the morning.

26

CHAR WAS SCRATCHING THEIR nails on the frame of the bunk, unable to sleep. I went over and sat beside them. We met like two friends lost in the night.

"What is it, Char?"

"It's Umphrey," Char said.

"Who's Umphrey?"

"This sly little weasel."

"I've never even heard of him."

"You wouldn't. He's the quiet type. He does what he's supposed to do."

"What is it then?"

"Umphrey just got a six-figure advance on his novel. He says he might drop out. He says he doesn't really need Take Creek now anyway."

"There, there," I said.

"His work is painful, not to mention super boring. He writes all that backyard family drama about nothing. It's perfect and marketable. I want to be happy for him, I really do. But I'm so mad. Why do the jerks always win?"

"Most of the time they do," I said. "But there are others that win, too."

"Umphrey says he's moving to LA now. He says he wants to

buy a BMW convertible. He says he'll have his picture taken in the BMW by the coast in the day's last light. It's unforgivable what he's done to the form. He's a total human slouch."

I rubbed Char's back as gently as I could, wanting them to know that I was here and I was going to stay here for as long as it took. I asked about their novel, how it was coming along. They let out this angsty cry.

"It's all lies," they said. "I haven't written a word in weeks. I called my mom for advice, but she's on another level. She says it's good for a young writer to get that vote of confidence, and that I shouldn't be upset with Umphrey."

"Maybe she has a point," I said.

"What does Mom know about writing?" Char said. "She's harvesting her winter crop in the garden, putting it all in a potato sack. The preternatural heads of cabbage. The Brussels sprouts. The cauliflower. The leafy bundles of dinosaur kale. The rain hasn't stopped in weeks where I come from. Mom says the planet is drowning in its own misery. I think she's drowning in a bottle of pinot noir. She knows jack-all about writing."

"What do you think it is?"

"What do you mean?"

"Why you're so mad," I said. "Why you can't work."

"It's a war in here. That's what it is. At Take Creek, everyone is bleeding and charging the field. The guns are drawn. The missiles are aimed."

"You're not the type to go throwing around war metaphors."

"It gets me heavy, that's all," Char said. "If Umphrey wins an award, I'll find him in his sun-filled, Hollywood flat, and I'll make sure he really squeals. Have you had anything to eat today? I'm starving."

We went to The Chow Hall and gorged on midnight muffuletta sandwiches. Then we ate three bowls of stracciatella apiece. Announcements were made on the overhead speaker warning us of a coming cold snap. There was a high-pressure system building in the Gulf of Mexico and we needed to stay on our toes. We nodded our heads and listened, assenting to whatever meaning we could find. I reached for my camera again. I collected the scraps on my tray into a pile. Char rested their head in their hands and sighed. Gregor walked up to the table with two Chicago dogs and a bucket of crushed ice.

"These dogs need no introduction," he said. "The bucket of ice, though. What do you think that's for?"

"I couldn't even guess," Char said.

"Whatever I want," Gregor said. "I just grab stuff even when there's no reason. Yesterday, a stack of napkins. The day before that, a frozen mop. I'm a seeker. I want to gather things and show them to people for what they are."

"And what's that?" I said.

"I don't know," Gregor said. "That's why I need your help. Have some ice. Both of you. Go on. Take a handful."

"Sorry," I said. "I'm really full right now."

"Don't be an ass, okay?"

We each took some ice and put it in our mouth and chewed.

"Where's Salter been by the way?" Gregor said. "I couldn't get through for over a month. This morning was the first I've seen him all semester."

"He went somewhere, Gregor."

"Like where? Like, he wandered into the jungle of war with a camera? Like, he met a good ol' western cowgirl and now he's shopping for a promise ring? Sixty grand a year I'm paying for this. Bullshit. That's what I say."

"You're not the only person dropping off," Char said. "I need to find a quiet place, too. Take Creek is losing its force for me. I can't keep waiting forever."

Gregor took a photograph of the food on his tray. He tried to talk to Char about their novel, but Char said it was a dead end and then they got up and left. I drummed my fingers on the table, unsure of what to say next.

"Are you still following for him?" Gregor said.

"What do you mean?" I said.

"I'm talking about Manning. Manning and whoever else. What's your assignment right now?"

"I need to get work ready for the big show," I said. "The agents are coming from New York. The editors. The curators. The reps from Magnum."

"You think you're alone here, don't you?"

"Of course I'm alone," I said. "We all are. That's the point."

"I have my own assignments for Salter," Gregor said. "So do the others. Why would you be any different?"

I looked across the table at Gregor, suddenly interested in what he meant.

"Are you following, too, Gregor?"

"Following what?" Gregor said. "The same subjects as you? I don't know. How do you figure?"

"That's impossible," I said. "You're just a braindead layabout from Ohio."

"We're pawns in the same move," Gregor said. "Don't you see that by now? We're being abused. We're walking around like dried-up has-beens in snow camo."

I scoffed.

"What do you know about snow camo?"

Gregor stood and stretched, wiping his face with his sleeve. He bent down and arched his hips. His dust-covered, old Yashica camera dangled from a rope around his neck. He pointed the lens at my hands, folded on the table, and shot. I wanted to tell him that I had once had a camera just like it, but didn't say a word.

"Mull it over," he said. "It makes sense. Char sees what's happening now. So does Jersey."

"Jersey operates on his own register. You don't get to make stupid sentences about Jersey."

"Jersey's a hack. But he has personality so you all revere him as a god."

"He's moving on anyway," I said. "And he's going to do something big. Meanwhile you'll be washing dishes in Williamsburg and wondering what you did with your life. I can already see it, Gregor. You'll be posting your resume online, digging around for the best photo for your profile. I bet that when the time comes you can't even get a job at the local craft supply store."

After Gregor left, I sat there for a while by myself, picking at pieces of wood flaking off the table, studying how the light fell straight down from the ceiling, as if pulled to the floor.

It was the week in which the Mayor of New York City went to Washington for a sit-down with the Joint Chiefs, the week a fluke cyclone devastated the Indian state of Kerala, taking more than ten thousand lives and leaving hundreds of thousands displaced.

All across campus we were drowning in conversation, the musings of idle talk. In the days to come I carried on shooting here and there, but mostly I was processing work from the break, honing in on this bleak aesthetic. Time lurched at the computer. Moments faded to the crackling of keys. Periodically the wind picked up and blew massive chunks of snow onto the roof. The building engineers stopped by to retape the windows. They climbed ladders, shoveled, cleared the gutters with tools shaped like ice cream scoops. I pretended I was hiding out in a dark, wet cave, paring my nails and reviewing footage from the cameras every hour. I kept watching but nothing, absolutely nothing, seemed to be happening in Manning's world. When he wanted to reach me, Salter left instructions under my pillow, indecipherable notes he tucked into an old pocket volume of Lorca.

27

Thursday morning I got the call from Magda at *The Lancer*.

"We're experiencing problems," she said.

"Problems how?" I said.

"We want to run a piece on you, but the timing isn't in our favor. It's a small formatting issue, a glitch."

"I don't understand."

"Your work is stunning, if you don't mind me saying."

"I appreciate that."

"These shots are like arrows. When I look at them I feel myself erased."

"Thanks."

"Thing is, we don't have a large enough readership, and it's only getting worse. We're looking for ways to peel back the page count. We need to work with less. We're learning to cull the extremities. In publishing now, it's not really a question of numbers, as it were. Nowadays, it's more about relationships. It's about your editors, their reputations, and who they know. Take *Sputum*, for example. Or even *Splishalings*. These folks are making out pretty well, in spite of the odds. That's because they have big-name editors, big-name contributors, and big-name readers. This gives them a level of buy-in that *The Lancer* could never be able to match. Plus there's the internet. That's one thing that isn't helping us in the slightest. *The Lancer* used to be premium niche publication. Notice that word. Niche. It connotes a self-awareness of place, an acceptance of certain limitations in the culture. We were never interested in trying to change the world with a single issue. We were just doing our part. That's all past tense now. We're slipping away, and there's nothing we can do to stop it. Do you want to know a tidbit about me? Here's a tidbit about me. I'm an unpublished poet. I bet you didn't know that. I don't regret taking it on, though I do wake up sometimes in the middle of the night dripping with sweat, soaking the sheets, wondering where I left my keys. I don't regret a single thing. I blew three marriages and four chances to be a decent mother. It's been a decent life. Truly, it has, although I never published a single word."

"I'm just happy there are people like you out there. It must be hard work, Magda. I hope it's okay for me to call you Magda."

"Magda is fine. So is Magpie. So is Mags, Magsie, Magdalena. Anything you want to call me is fine."

"I'll remember that."

"We truly enjoyed your submission, and while it's not the best fit for *The Lancer* right now, we hope you'll think of us in the future. We'd be interested in seeing others. I want you to know that we take every submission seriously."

"I've never been rejected over the phone. I can't believe you're taking the time to call me."

"I try to come at this on a more personal level. It matters to me. I have an intern named Milly. She liked your work. She has a magical eye. Milly helps me sort through the slush. She also helps me organize the proofs when we get ready to go to print. Milly is still in high school. She'll be a junior next year. One day she hopes to go to Take Creek like you."

"I hope she gets what she wants."

"I'm sure you'll find a mention soon. I don't doubt it for a minute."

"I recently applied for a residency in Wyoming. Two weeks on a ranch in the middle of nowhere. Two weeks to work constantly without interruption. It didn't pan out."

There was a pause on the line.

"Don't get sad," Magda said.

"I'm not. Really, I'm not. Where are you calling from, by the way?"

"Albuquerque, New Mexico. The Land of Enchantment. It's a gloriously clear, sunny day. Chilly but dry. Snow on the peaks. The color of a watermelon when it wants to be. Just a hundred or so miles from here, D.H. Lawrence used to cook dinner over an open fire and drink wine with his friends. Don't let anything slight stop you, son. Most of the other stuff doesn't really matter anyway."

I went to The Farley Gardens and sat on a bench. A lone white-tail doe trod across the brackens. Squirrels darted in and out of their dens, digging up nuts and seeds from nearby caches. I leaned back and thought about my submission, only to realize that I couldn't even remember what I had submitted in the first place. All I knew for certain was that soon the vines around me would blossom into dense purpleblue flowers and Salter would sit us down on the floor of the basement and order us to go out into the bloom to take photographs of flowers that didn't look like photographs of flowers.

That afternoon, Franny and I found ourselves dangling by The Barn again, absorbed in a rare bout of intense February sun. Invariably, the air today had a weight to it, a habit of clinging to our clothes. We inhaled deeply from the nameless bioorganic steam of wet livestock, fresh shit, and rotten feed that drifted out of The Barn like a raging plume of smoke, coursing downwind and settling, eventually, on the exact spot where we lay. Add to this the lackluster scenery and the unremarkable—even unsightly—job of the landscaping, and the end result was a win: a pair of hammocks that no one dared to dangle in and save us.

We were each smoking our own spliff, talking through a batch of laconic moves in Franny's latest project.

"I need your honest opinion," she said.

"I don't know how to form one. It's not in my vocabulary. I barely understand what you're saying right now."

"Don't be coy. You have nice taste."

"Wow," I said. "What a compliment. Nice taste. Prim fellow. Good heart. It's what I've always wanted."

"I haven't watched a movie in over two and a half weeks. Zoe has me back on the horse. There isn't any time for film. I'm not asking you to say congratulations. I'm just keeping you in the loop."

"I never said there was anything wrong with watching movies all day."

"I know," Franny said. "But it's as if I've crawled out of the basement somewhere. I was getting down. The only place to go was deeper. I wanted to know what it felt like to be there. Is that crazy? Is wanting to know the lowest place you can go crazy or isn't it? It doesn't matter now. But thanks for not holding it against me."

"I want to have sex with you in a barn that doesn't smell like a slaughterhouse. I want sex on last year's bales of hay, with all the moans and the grunts. I want you screaming at the local foliage."

"We can't get away with that here," Franny said. "Sex at Take Creek is like sex at church. I'm tiptoeing around. I'm pretending like it's not my thing. Meanwhile it just keeps building up. I wonder what they're serving for dinner."

We dangled like that for the rest of the afternoon, approximating some fleeting version of ourselves. We smoked. We napped. We rolled around. We laughed. Then we spoke through the stuff that was missing. Her family in California. A holiday spent on the Russian River. Drinking beer. Sleeping late. Listening to the rain. Taking a stab at the largest crossword puzzle she had ever seen. The banality of life was never lost on her. I listened and drank carrot juice from a mason jar, licking the sweetness off my teeth as she spoke. Just then a farmhand named Roge walked by and gave us a chintzy, one-fingered wave. He carried his scythe down the path and made a sharp left for the Quonset huts full of hay.

It was in this moment, right when I was about to ask Franny for another spliff, that we first heard the helicopter. We didn't know it was a helicopter then. We only knew it as a distant droning whir that cut the quiet of the day to pieces. The noise of the thing grew louder as it neared, so we stood up and started walking, not sure where we were going but doing our best to follow the sound, as if we thought we could somehow meet the sound in the middle. We stopped at the edge of The Quad and looked up as the helicopter came into view. Franny walked over closer, filling in where the others were forming, a large mass of Take Creek bodies, with every contingent accounted for, from the cooks to the higher-ups, the bus drivers to the professors, the students to the part-time librarians. We all poured out onto The Quad, curious to see what was afoot. I stayed back and shot a roll of Tri-X 400 pushed to 800, a grainy film that could withstand a good deal of manipulation. I took Roge's picture just as he turned the corner with his scythe. Moments later, I shot Zoe and Salter running over like concerned parents, approaching an event they couldn't explain. Everyone was talking then, coming outside and forming a swelling hive between the buildings. The helicopter landed in a far corner of The Quad. It kicked up so much snow that visibility went to less than a few feet. The rotors roared on. We couldn't see the people in front of us or behind us. We reached out with our hands, touching the backs and arms of whomever was closest, letting them know we were there. I covered my eyes from the swirling white cloud. A little while later, the sound shifted, although not in a way I could describe. I craned my neck just in time to see the helicopter rising slowly into the air, above the snow, above Take Creek, before turning south and flying off. I pushed to the front of the crowd, where I found Franny collapsed to her knees, gazing out in the same direction as everyone else. Todd Mackintosh and Jasmine Fincher stood beside her, holding hands and praying. The snow settled like dust at our feet. The sky opened in bluewhite strokes. Out at the periphery, a solitary figure appeared with two large trunks of luggage and waved. I raised the camera to my eye, but didn't shoot. It was him. Manning was back.

28

MARY FRANKEL ENTERED STAGE right wearing a checkered yellow cardigan, torn cargo pants, knee-high galoshes, and a purple sash flung over her shoulder. Her face was paler than any photograph, spotted red and tight at the jaw. The ashen, frizzy hair by which we all knew her—from magazines, books, profiles, lectures—bounced atop her head like a dense, shaking bush. I sat alone in the middle of the house, hunched over, pretending to take notes. Mary Frankel grabbed the microphone and peered out across the audience.

"Thanks for coming on such a cold night. I appreciate your being here. I'm sorry I couldn't make it sooner. I was delayed in Kabul, then again in Istanbul, then again in Frankfurt. But that's just the life of the road, isn't it? Entire days seem to vanish in transit. Our bodies slow. Our thoughts drift. In transit, we are other than ourselves, and maybe doubled. In transit, we are beaten down, thirsty, sleepless, maimed. Our ankles swell. Our noses go runny. Our eyes gloss over as we stare up at the nearest screen, scanning for updates, changes in status, location, equipment. There's no remedy for our breath either. In transit, everything is rotting, everything reeks. We're no exception. We're a bony bag of garbage left out on the concourse. The lights can't be turned off. The water doesn't get any warmer. The chairs never soften. The windows can't be opened. Nothing changes in transit except for the time passing by, moment to moment, counting the seconds, waiting. In transit, there is only waiting. The persistent selfsameness of waiting. Here, perhaps more than anywhere else, we are forced to stop and sit down, to consider the nature of our collective situation. The known world becomes like a playpen in the other room, a destination we'll never get to, even though we're hurtling toward it with all our might. By the time I made it to New York, it was two forty-five in the morning. I took a room by the airport and booked a seat on the first flight out. Then they lost my luggage. Further delays ensued. More waiting. A day later, I was rerouted through Boston, but a freak storm grounded flights at Logan for over thirty-six hours, so the story dragged on. I was told I'd have to wait longer, to accept the things I couldn't change. Two days later, I finally touched down upstate with the cold coffee and the uneaten overpriced sandwich, the soggy tomato, the malformed lettuce, the mealy apple lost among half-empty water bottles and shed layers at the bottom of the bag. That was this morning around eight fifteen. I spent the day with some of your professors, and I have to say, you folks have it good here. You're setting an example for the rest of us, paving the way for those who come next. Which begs the question. Have you ever dreamed of doing something, but then stopped short of pursuing it because it just seemed too hard? Yeah, I know. I almost quit. If I could count the number of times I almost put down my camera and caught the next flight home, I would. Once, while on leave in the Azores, my masseuse plopped his erect member right into the palm of my hand. A few weeks later, I shot Ethiopian Jews being airlifted to Israel. A few weeks after that, I flew to Iraq through Lebanon, my tenth visit in three months. It was a frenzied year. They wanted us everywhere at once. But it wasn't like that where I started. No, no. That was a much slower time, in Smyrna, Tennessee, which is full of other kinds of happenings, most of them quite unholy. For example, one day, I walked into the barn and found my Aunt Bev hanging from a rope tied to a rafter. Another day, I watched Mama raise the hatchet and kill our beloved dog, Thaddeus, when he turned on her in the yellow pasture. I was too young when I found Aunt Bev, maybe eleven, maybe twelve. It was the first dead body I ever saw. I don't remember if it smelled or not. I didn't have a camera. It was a much slower time, in the Sun Belt, where I come from. I grew up like the rest of them there, faring for what I could. Years floated by like broken centuries. One day, I was maybe eleven, maybe twelve, and the next day, I was twenty. I was spending too much time at the river, chasing a boy named Charles, and training to be a TIG welder. Fast forward forty-four years, and here I am today, a war photographer, and sometimes a teacher, meaning I get paid to talk when people want to hear me. Over the years I documented conflict in El Salvador, Nicaragua, the United States, Lebanon, Yemen, Guatemala, the West Bank, Gaza, Israel, India, Sri Lanka, Pakistan, Indonesia, Afghanistan, Iran, Somalia, Egypt, Libya, Sudan, Ethiopia, the DRC, Mali, Madagascar, Bosnia, Kosovo, Chechnya, Russia, Tajikistan, Georgia, Mexico, Brazil, Paraguay, Colombia, Venezuela, and more. I'd like to think my work bears witness to the evils of humanity, and functions as a humble testimony about what goes on down here. Though it's not just a testimony for us, it's also a testimony for God Himself, whom I someday hope to meet, interrogate, and torture with every fiber of my being. Until then, I carry around the camera and I shoot so people never forget. I keep the zeitgeist raging like Hosea's golden tongue. But let's get back to the beginning, the putting a welder to photography. On my twenty-second birthday I bought my first camera. I didn't have any real reason to buy one. I just bought it out of curiosity. I taught myself how to use it and I took it with me everywhere. Six months later, I met a man in Nashville named Granger, a deadbeat drunk with an impressive collection of cameras and his very own darkroom. Granger taught me how to process and print my shots, most of which depicted the nobodies I saw roaming around Smyrna and other towns, people without jobs, without hopes, without anywhere to be. These people held sad hats and squatted by the road, waiting for work. They wailed their tunes. They begged for change on the corner, totally blind. One day, Granger went behind my back and sent some of this work to an editor at *Life*. Nothing would ever be the same. My first assignment sent me to Northern Ireland, my second to Kashmir. After that, I took my cameras and boarded a plane for Afghanistan, where I documented the mujahideen fighting the Soviets. I almost lost my mind that year in the mountains. I barely came home in my body. But the work I did there led to a major breakthrough, and my first solo show in San Francisco. That year taught me a thing or two about process, about getting to work every day, about walking out and making a mess of it, and learning how to harness the energy of God. This is another line I'm talking about when I'm talking about war. There's the war out there, but there's also the war in here, inside the human heart, the weak mind, disassembling, soft as an egg, moping around the window, sheepish, derelict, spotting the shadows of passersby on the street. I never told you about the demons, did I? I never told you about how to talk back to them when they're breathing down your neck. Which begs the question. Do you believe we have to confront death itself in order to finally say yes to our impulses? Well, I do. I damn well do. Once upon a time, I was on a plane heading from Karachi to Peshawar, and both engines went out. We fell ten thousand feet in less than a minute. Everyone was screaming. Everyone was praying. Just shy of the mountains, the engines fired up and the pilots regained control of the plane. After that flight, I didn't even sleep without a camera in my hand. I vowed to never doubt the course of rivers. I'm a lucky woman. I'm an angel chosen by God to represent reality. And here's what I want for you. I want you to cut out a hole in your chest and tell me what you see there. What I see is blood, flesh, slimy organs, sacks of fluid. But you see something else. No one sees it but you. Hitler, too, wanted to become an artist. He really did. But he gave up when his paintings didn't get him into art school in Vienna. Look what he did instead. Don't give up, is what

I'm saying. Don't let anyone tell you what is and isn't possible. Everywhere we look, we see signs and messages telling us to stop. Don't let yourself be distracted. You need to keep doing your language. Anyone who tells you otherwise is full of shit, and I suspect they themselves will one day turn on you as well. You are at war. Make no mistake. Will you be killed or will you fight to the death? That's the question. I myself chose to fight. I'm still fighting now, and I'll still be fighting then. It's the code of the warrior. I took a few partners along the way, made a few nice friends, but most people ended up trying to break me down, to sabotage me. I thought these people were trying to help, but they weren't. They were drowning me in their own fury. I flew them. I even let a couple circle around me like vultures. That was maybe fine, but I can't say for sure. I just kept sitting down to do my work, I kept following the story, I kept looking through the lens, I kept reaching for that next shot. Don't get me wrong. The war stops for nothing save death. It's going to eat up your entire life. While the war is full of its own challenges, I hope you come to realize that in your deepest moments of doubt and self-pity the only thing more depressing than carrying on is sitting back and letting the war slide by you like a slick of lost oil on a fast-moving Tennessee stream. Who are you? Why are you here? What is the meaning of your life? From where I'm standing, the answer seems quite clear. The meaning of your life lies not in something beyond you, but rather inside of you, in your passions, in how you live those passions in your daily experience. History makes us numb if we're not careful. Don't let's get numb. Shoot on. Dance a jig. Sculpt your bronze. I can see some of your faces right now, and I have to tell you, it's my first time to Take Creek and I can't decide which way is up. This place is a firestorm. It's a sick fantasy. I've never heard so many young people whining in all my life. Stop your whining. Try to be grateful you're not hungry in someone else's bunker begging for a light. And when you get out, which I hope you all do, be sure to remember what you did here and why you did it, and then be sure to invest ten to fifteen percent of your take-home earnings in a reputable S&P Index Fund for the remainder of your lovely little stateside life and let the spirit of the thing grow like a flower. Praise Jesus. Save the whales. Look out for landmines. My name is Mary Frankel and I approve this message."

I followed Gregor out the door and down the stairs and we smoked a spliff behind a nearby tree. We didn't say much or fix our eyes on the given horizon. The snow kept falling in fitful bursts, scattering like cinders on the steps. Over by The Library a group of students gathered for a game of football in their underwear, calling out plays in Modern Greek. It was a running game mostly, eight freezing bodies all clung together, pummeling back and forth across the lawn, hitting their way through the snow.

After a while The Shaker emptied out, the houselights dimmed, and Gregor wandered off into the darkness. I shot him as he disappeared, bundled up, bearing it away, the lone figure leaning forward into night. Mary Frankel walked out and made her way down the stairs onto the path. I stepped into the light and approached her just as she removed her ashen frizzy wig. She scratched at her bald scalp and lit a stubby unfiltered cigarette.

"I'd appreciate if you didn't tell anyone what you just saw," she said. "I'm keeping it to myself, hurtling toward my own destination."

"I don't exactly know what I saw," I said.

"I have cancer, you idiot. It's in my ovaries and it's reaching out to say hello to all my other special parts. I won't tell it my name until I have to."

"You're still blazing along."

"I've been working for almost fifty years. Do you think I want to go home to die at some lake house? I do not. Nothing sounds worse. I'd rather die on assignment. Speaking of, when did Sol Lewitt do the drawing in The Library? The angles make no sense."

"Jersey says that the drawing signals the end of sense and the beginning of something else."

"People are dying, naked, starving, hysterical. They need us to do something. Then Sol Lewitt walks into the room and draws a squiggly line across the wall and all of you art school wonks think the earth just became a square. You and your cronies are crazy. I'm on the next flight out."

"Before you leave, can I ask for your advice?"

"It's not worth much, but I'm listening."

"Have you ever shot with anything besides a camera? I mean, have you ever really shot someone?"

"The force of law, you're talking."

"Shooting with anything besides a camera. Have you?"

"I think so, but I don't remember the specifics," Mary said. "I have a distinct memory of holding a gun over someone, then pressing the end of the barrel on their forehead between the eyes. Other than that, it's a blank. Maybe it happened. Maybe it didn't. I can't fill in the picture by myself. I'd need a witness. In war, a reliable witness is hard to come by."

"Have you ever tailed anyone?"

"Sure."

"I mean covert."

"Hundreds of times, maybe thousands. What's your beat?"

"It's my professor."

"Jimmy Salter," Mary said. "He comes across like an unemployed alcoholic or broken diplomat. He speaks in a lawless dialect."

"He has me tailing a fellow student, this rising star from Mallorca."

"Now that's a beautiful island."

"At first, I followed him in person, but then I was found out."

"It's a confined environment. There are a limited number of players. There's nowhere to hide. The rules of engagement are exact."

"Salter told me to find a way to keep following no matter what, but I had no plan. Then he mailed me a box of cameras."

"The plot thickens."

"I installed them all over campus," I said. "And now I'm supposed to tell him what I find."

"Sounds interesting. Where do I come in?"

"This student, my target, he's been back for almost a week now. I'm watching everything he does. I see him from every angle. I can't find the story, though."

"Perhaps you should invent one," Mary said.

I looked at her.

"Invent one how?" I said.

"I don't know, just make something up. Thread together a few shots and tell a story. That's all we're really capable of anyway. Taking pieces. Putting them in order. That's your job. Not to mention he's your professor, and you're his student. Unless you want to go home or be a fussbucket, you have to do what he says. This place is bonkers. You folks are floating in the clouds."

"Have you had a chance to check out the installations on campus? The work here is world class."

"For me, art happens in the street," Mary said. "Not in galleries or museums. And certainly not on campus at private schools like this. It's not an argument. I'm not trying to get a rise out of you. It's just my take on things."

Mary pinched the cigarette at its tip, rolling it between her fingers until the cherry fell to the ground. I asked what she was doing.

"It's called field dressing," she said. "You have to put out your cigarette, but you don't want to leave the butt behind because if your enemies see it, they'll know you were there. Leave no trace. Tread lightly on the battlefield."

"Do you really believe all this talk about war?" I said.

"Of course not," she said. "But the audience eats it up. They love it. They want maximum potential. That's what war, and the concept of war, delivers. It's an opportunity to sit back and think about death, which I don't really do, by the way. If I spent all that time thinking about death, I have to say I wouldn't get much done."

"Who are your favorite shooters?"

"I hate that question, so I'll pretend like you never asked it."

"What about the iPhone?"

"If I were you, I'd start shooting on that thing right away. It's going to displace the traditional camera. You should figure out why."

"I should just make something up then."

"Thread together a few shots and tell Salter that Manning is a secret agent for Mossad carrying out orders from a rogue sect in Haifa. There's an example. It's the first thing that came to mind. Tell him this student is an informant. Tell him he works for the mob. It doesn't matter what you say, as long as the story is compelling."

"But what about you?"

"What about me?" Mary said.

"Does that mean you're just telling stories, too?"

She lit another cigarette and looked down at her galoshes.

"You seem like smart folks," she said. "I'm sure you'll find the answers to those questions on your own. Meanwhile, you should just keep doing the motions so you can get out of here. You need to get out of here as soon as possible."

When Mary Frankel was gone, I went back inside The Shaker and perused the walls, checking out her recent work from Syria, which was on display until the end of the week. These were not your typical photographs of war. They were four-foot-by-six-foot digital C-prints shot on a large-format camera with infrared color film. Deep purples and reds dominated the scenes, giving the conflict an otherworldly, almost hypnotic effect. Here was a story about war, struggle, and human evil, but Mary Frankel was telling it in a new language.

In one shot, a woman held her child to her chest in a sublime pink, while behind her the magnetic red sky framed a city of blown-out buildings and streets stacked high with rubble. A tank approached in the distance, its flag impossible to identify. In the bottom right corner, near the woman's callused bare feet, a flower blossomed out of a pile of rocks. The rocks were surrounded by egg white shell casings. The sun burned a smoky blue.

29

I WENT TO OFFICE hours to talk about my progress.

"You're the resident beast, kid. But your approach suggests tired. It stinks of fatigue and wanting. Marching out of the cold like that, carrying around a rangefinder and wishing you weren't. Where's your iPhone?"

"In my pocket."

"That's what I thought. I trust you found a couple takeaways in the Frankel visit. She's a piece of work and pretty tired herself, from what I hear."

"I've never met anyone like her. She's a real shooter."

"Indeed. The kind you don't come by much anymore. Back in my day, that was what you went for. An absolutely taut framework. Nowadays it's plastic. Shooters shift with every post. They don't have honor. Not Mary Frankel. Mary Frankel has honor. Mary Frankel is loyal. Mary Frankel has fidelity. She's the type who thinks about blowing up the Pentagon. And probably for the right reasons, too. I'm watching our boy day and night on The Nodes. You did good work with the install. I commend good work. I value good work. Clearly you followed my instructions."

"I've been watching. There's nothing of interest yet. Manning is in retreat, going through an ascetic phase."

"And?"

"I'm hearing rumors."

"Of a war? An uprising? A fleeting change in consciousness? What?"

"He may have gone to Israel before he boarded the art boat."

"Israel? The art boat? You're talking Mandarin to me. Speak English, would you?"

"I'm still working out the kinks. I need more time. I heard he came back with acid. A lot of acid. He's taking it every day. He says it's helping him focus."

"I like that, kid. He's traipsing around searching for signs. He's acting like a French philosopher driving around the wastelands of Nevada. Meanwhile we're out here in the digisphere waiting for him to trip on a twig. You and I are playing God with these cameras. We're pushing the limits. Have you spoken to anyone about our activities?"

"Of course not."

"Don't lie to me, kid."

"It's just us. I promise."

"It has to stay that way. Otherwise, you get the boot, and I have to find a new line of work. Bad news, maybe."

"I'm not really comfortable watching. I feel like a voyeur."

"That's the most pathetic thing. The American lackey speaks. His candor is dumb and predictable."

"I'm not kidding. When I watch The Nodes for too long, it induces a neurosis in me, a variety of schizophrenia. Is this a normal response?"

"Don't pretend to be surprised. Photography has always been linked to surveillance. We've been spying on each other for nearly two hundred years. It's inherent to the form. Grandma knew it even though she never trusted photography and was maybe even scared by it. Most of the great work of the moderns sheds light on the same point. The shooter. The camera. Roaming around. Flickering in secret. From the hip. At the window. Behind the wall. It's just a reordering we're talking about now. Plus, we have the world of digitization, so we've moved into the plane of something far more immediate. Just keep watching what you see. I have a hunch that if this wombat takes enough dope one night we'll catch a show we'll never forget. You still haven't read Spinoza, have you?"

"No."

"And you still haven't tasted bitter melon?"

"No."

"You need to approach Manning soon, but you need to do so with caution. I'll be out of pocket for the next few days. Frankel's shots go to a gallery in New York for a fundraiser to raise awareness about human rights. She asked if I'd come down and say a word or two about her work. I don't mind really. I can do my part. Out in the desert, I went rogue. I fasted. I feasted. I went on a seventeen-mile hike. It was enough quiet to make the city actually appealing. What did you learn about Jillian Arcadia?"

"She may be the one. I don't know."

"That's what I heard from Jim, too."

"Her work is perplexing. It goes beyond the normal vocabulary. We cased around and took in the sights. Everywhere we went, it was freezing. The motels were empty. The sculptures and installations couldn't be classified. Jersey was writing the whole time. It's an ode to Chairman Mao. I've seen a rough draft. It can't be classified, either."

"Your friend is writing. I know. Everyone knows. The whole campus is talking about it. Some of the higher-ups predict that in ten or twenty years he'll occupy a significant position among the New York literati. I have my doubts, but no one cares. They say I know nothing about literature. I say they know nothing, period."

"I was going to shoot Arcadia's work, but I ended up just shooting the weather in various poses. The new work is naturalistic. It marks my first turn inward."

"Your first turn inward? That's your batty ego talking and you know it. Let me see the shots, kid."

"This first one is a clump of ice behind a gas station."

"Hey, what's this?"

"That's snow."

"No, it's not. It's heavenly. Who shot this?"

"I did."

"That's impossible."

"It was me."

"When?"

"In Coventry. We were walking at dusk, casing out The Frost House."

"Robert Frost?"

"Right."

"I hate Robert Frost."

"Right."

"What were you doing there?"

"Checking out another Jillian Arcadia installation. We couldn't get in, though. After that things went downhill fast."

"Not only is this shot not total deershit. It's masterful. How did you achieve it?"

"I just shot what I saw. In the instant. Out of nowhere. A random occurrence."

"There's a technical difficulty to shooting things like clouds, snow, water, et cetera. Every photographer obsesses over it. What you're up to here is different. I smell a lucid, hungry-eyed beast."

"I appreciate that."

"I can't believe I'm saying it. Cut out my tongue and feed it to the wolves, kid. I want you to blow this up. I want to see it glowing on the wall, the size of a medium window. Finally you have a proof worth spitting on. Finally there's a reason to keep shaking at the light. You should be proud of yourself. Most people never get a shot like this. And if they do, they get it once. The trick is to get it twice, and then to get it again and again until you croak. Have I made myself clear?"

30

EVERYWHERE WE WENT THAT winter the concept of parallax kept popping up in our lives. I could hear the word when I woke. I could feel it worming around the roof of my mouth. Sometimes I could even see it in the snow, in hidden messages, in tracings, in the bloated symbols of a foreign script.

Salter said that cunning was the first act.

Salter said that perspective donned the face of truth, but it abided by the most fateful of human rituals.

Lens craft.

Light craft.

Cauterizations of existing forms.

The Nodes burned holes in my eyeballs. I watched nothing happen over and over, day after day, week after week, footage of Manning pacing about his studio, on acid, obsessed with the objects around him and focused on the arrangement of those objects in the room.

A stack of folded sweaters and corduroy pants. His pea coat. His cameras. His paints. His brushes. His snowboots. His sketch-books. His tools. His dropcloths. A few rolls of canvas. A milk crate full of scrap metal. A cardboard box full of scrap wood.

Manning would gather all these objects on the table as if he were arranging a still life, only to then, seconds later, up and move them somewhere else. Sometimes he put everything back in the place it was before. Other times, he moved each object to a new place. Once in a while, he even went so far as to hide certain objects—a dowel saw, a calculator, a tube of toothpaste—though I could never figure out who he was hiding them from, or why he was hiding them at all.

At some point, February gave way to March. The days grew longer, but it was impossible to register how. The snow kept coming, the temps kept falling. Even the wind made sounds like language. I read less, I shot less. I slept more, I ate more. I stopped answering calls from family. My face began to swell when exposed to too much light. I showered every morning and shaved every night before bed, mirroring my habits on advice gleaned from an unpublished notebook attributed to Garry Winogrand. Isolation reigned. I was smoking twice the usual amount.

The most recent voicemail from my father was quasi-distressing.

"Your silence is giving your mother and me a real heartache. Why won't you speak to us, son? Have we done something to upset you? Your mother is convinced it's her fault. She dropped you when you were a baby. She says she knew it'd come back to haunt her. We missed you at Christmas. Your brother came down with his new fiancée. Her name is Tamela. Like Pamela but with a T. She knows how to spill her guts after a few too many drinks, but your mother and I are happy for Paul. He's growing his hair out, practicing the banjo. He opened three more Subways, so business must be good. Anyway, we hope you know that we're thinking about you. We're proud of the person you're becoming. We'd love to hear what you're learning this semester. We miss the Sunday calls. If you get a chance, even a couple of spare minutes, give us a ring, and let us know you're okay. We're praying for you. May God speed you on your journey into His Everlong and Lasting Light."

Friday afternoon, I got up the nerve to visit Manning for the first time since the break. When I walked into his studio he was lying on his side on a pillow, naked and shivering, breathing heavily through his nose. I closed the door, took off my hat and jacket, and kneeled down beside him on the floor. Although I had been watching him closely on camera, being there in the frame with him felt stranger than I had imagined it would.

The walls were empty and freshly painted white. Manning's supplies were stashed in the corner on a moving blanket. Manning poured a glass of water from a pitcher, drinking it in small sips, wetting his lips. I rested my hand on his shoulder. He brushed me off. He grabbed a beach towel off the chair, draped it over his lap like a rag, and lit a votive candle with a match, putting it out on his tongue. His white noise machine was on full blast then. A smudge stick of sage burned on a porcelain plate.

Finally, he texted me: WHAT GIVES?

I looked up, taking this as a sign he was ready to speak. I reached for my phone and started typing.

Me: Are the rumors true?

Him: Yes. When I first returned it was exactly what I wanted. I arrived like the body of a dead sultan coming out of a hospital. But then there was the acid. I was dosing a lot. A couple of days ago, it fell apart. I fell apart. I hit the psychosocial wall. When I woke up the next afternoon I took a vow of silence. I haven't spoken since. I need to reflect on the world around me. I've spent too long measuring other people's time.

Me: I was there. I stood there on the edge of The Quad and watched you walk through the crowd. Everyone was talking then, coming outside, and assembling around you in solemn confirmation. You're still not speaking to anyone?

Him: That's true.

Manning uncrossed and stretched out his legs, reaching for a small pocket of sunlight, inching his body slantwise across the floor. It looked like he had lost twenty or thirty pounds. His skin was flaky and lifeless, stamped like a muted luster. He held his phone in his hand. I waited. He wanted me to write back with more.

Me: Are they all coming to see you?

Him: You're the third.

Me: Are you receiving everyone?

Him: I'm refusing most everyone.

Me: Does this mean your show is off?

Manning shrugged his shoulders, laughing. He opened a can of snus and put a pinch into his mouth, forming it into a ball on the inside of his lip.

Him: There is no show. I told the higher-ups.

Me: You like snus now?

Him: I never stopped liking snus. It was just temporarily unavailable. I procured more on my voyage. What do you care anyway?

A short period of silence took shape between us. It was the kind of break in conversation that revealed what was and wasn't being said. There was a lingering question buried inside the banter.

Him: Are you still following me?

Me: Following you how? You're not going out. You're cloistered up in here. No, I let that go. It was just a game anyway.

Manning poured more water and drank. He stood up and let the towel fall to the floor, bending at the waist. He looked at me and began writing again.

Him: Is the photograph ultimately by or about?

Me: Say that again.

Him: Is your photograph of the snow a photograph about the snow or a photograph by you?

Me: How do you know about the snow shot?

Him: Word travels fast in this township.

Me: How long are you going to go on with this silence?

Him: Not sure.

Me: We're texting, though, aren't we?

Him: Not sure.

I went to The Chow Hall for vegan steak au poivre and ate at a corner table by myself. I walked up for seconds, which turned into a motherlode of an end cut and a heaping spoonful of mashed potatoes. I met Peter Delacroix back at the table, blowing on his tea, coming in from the cold.

"Amazon will deliver here with drones soon," he said. "Hopefully that will change everything."

"Define everything, Peter."

"Change is constant. The one certainty in this life."

"Tell me about your latest script," I said.

"The newest project is a TV pilot. It's only two minutes long. Each episode is two minutes long. The main character is named Trevender. He's a juggler. Each episode is one of his acts. They're all different. The setting. The mood. The lighting. The circumstance. Trevender roams from town to town and lives off what he makes in his hat. The show is a tribute to buskers around the globe, people who hustle to get by on street corners just to keep throwing. Every episode is different. It's about juggling."

"Jersey also did a piece about a juggler."

"This one is more about the economy actually. The juggling is just a segue to talk about online consumption."

"How many episodes have you written?"

"Not a word. But the idea is totally formed in my head. I only need to find the time to sit down and write it. What is that?"

Peter pointed at my plate.

"Vegan steak au poivre," I said, cutting off a piece and offering him a bite. "I can barely tell the difference. It still bleeds on the plate."

"That's commerce for you, my friend," Peter said. "I ordered a new pair of slippers a few hours ago. I can't wait until they just fall from the sky."

Jersey walked over carrying a backpack full of energy bars. He gave us each one and sat down at the table.

"My hands are getting stronger," he said. "The same goes for my footwork, my placement, and my routes. Climbing is the perfect exercise for a writer. The world goes quiet on the wall. There's nothing but the moves. The simple grace of the ascent."

"What about this novel?" Peter said.

"It isn't a novel," Jersey said. "It's a hybrid form inspired by Chairman Mao. Novels are the province of egotistical losers. They're ideological tools. And they're passe, too."

"Did Chairman Mao say that?" Peter said.

"I don't know diddly about what Chairman Mao said," Jersey said.

"A billion people care," Peter said.

"That's so slight," Jersey said. "You're misreading the guy. You're also misreading the billion people. Chairman Mao was up to bigger business than just quoting himself. What is that?"

Jersey pointed at my plate.

"It's vegan steak au poivre," I said.

"That's disgusting," Jersey said, opening one of his energy bars and taking a wolfy bite. "You should snack on these. We're talking like seventy grams of protein in a single bar. I need that protein for muscle regeneration after my workouts."

"One could argue that climbing indoors isn't really climbing," Peter said.

Jersey wound up like he was about to go in for a slap. Peter flinched and then covered his face.

"I should start a small fire with your hair," Jersey said, and turned to me. "Do I look bulkier to you?"

"Bulkier how?"

"Bulkier like muscles," Jersey said. "Like cut. Like swoll. Like pump. Bulkier like this is a ripped glowing body."

"Maybe a little," I said. "I'm not sure, though."

Jersey gestured at Peter and flexed his forearm. Then he gestured at me.

"Why aren't you eating your bar?" he said.

"I'm stuffed," I said. "This is my second steak."

Jersey quickly grabbed my bar off the table and put it in his backpack with the others.

"Fine," he said. "More for me. What's with you lately anyway?"

"What do you mean?" I said.

"You seem like you're gone. I barely see you. I can't get through to you. You're always in the basement on the computer."

"It's just the usual work," I said. "But Salter says I hit the bullseye. I'm editing this shot of the snow, one of the shots from break. I'm going to blow it up. He says it's a wall-worthy image."

"How big?" Jersey said.

"The size of a medium window," I said.

"So still pretty small then, more or less."

"I'm entering a new phase," I said. "I'm turning inward."

"Check it out," Peter said, nudging Jersey. "Take Creek is full of surprises."

A group of students walked into The Chow Hall in their underwear. Most of them I didn't recognize. At the front was Margot Dansk holding a football. She called out a play in Modern Greek and everyone stormed the buffet for chow. Peter was amused by this spectacle, so he went over and asked what they were up to. Jersey and I stayed at the table and watched, looking on as the players loaded their trays, grunting from dish to dish, hitting each other by the chai bar in their skivvies.

"What just occurred here?" I said.

"A clan has formed," Jersey said. "And the game is their passion. I'm sure you've seen them practicing"

"Do they have a name?"

"They're the Wild Dogs. Every night at seven, they gather on the lawn by The Library. They're actively recruiting."

"I saw them playing after the Frankel lecture. I never imagined it would become a thing, though."

"Oh, it's a thing all right. Get a read on Peter right now. He's over there talking about Amazon. But give it a week or two, and he'll be on the team. I guarantee you. It's the feeling of being a part of a unit, a context beyond the self. That's what the team provides. Take Creek gets lonely. The team makes it easier to bear."

"You have something against football?" I said.

"I used to play actually," Jersey said. "I was a second-string punter. We won regionals one year and I was there. I never even got off the bench."

"I can't render the image," I said.

Jersey popped up and intimated a punt at the end of the table.

"It's a beautiful game," he said. "But it turns the world around in all the wrong ways. Except for when you're playing out in the weather like the Wild Dogs. Now that's a purer form of the game. That's play just for the sake of play. Pure play. At least for now. My gut tells me this will get weird. I bet the team continues to grow. A couple of weeks ago, they were only eight, and really quiet about the whole thing. That's changing. The organization. The candor. The volume. Are you still following for Salter?"

"The assignment shifted," I said. "It's more surveillance now."

"I still haven't seen Manning yet."

"I just went for a visit."

"And?" Jersey said.

"He's completely gone off the rails."

"What about the show?"

"He's taken a vow of silence. He's cooped up in his studio, naked, lit by a candle. It's like a scene from one of Franny's Polish movies. The show isn't happening. We can all forget about it."

"My offer to help still stands, you know."

I crumpled my napkin into a wad and dropped it onto my plate.

"I appreciate that," I said. "But I think I need to see this through on my own."

Over by the yogurt rack and the cold-pressed juice cooler, an underweight dancer named Jeremy Maynard slapped a painter named Millie Guy from behind. She flew into a rage. Jeremy threw a punch then. Millie dropped to her knees and dodged it. Jeremy charged, tackling Millie into the turnstile next to the kettle chip bowl and beating her face with a ladle. Kettle chips went flying. The entire team rushed over to break up the fight. Jersey counted the players one by one as they separated, and then shook his head in worry. He grabbed my camera off the table and took my picture, laughing.

"They're a wily gang of twenty-four now," he said. "So long as you count Peter Delacroix, too."

31

THE WAR SIRENS WENT off at three in the morning, waking us from our apoplectic slumber. Char took my hand and led me into the darkness. We followed the others across the entire eastern half of Take Creek, beyond The Chow Hall, The Shaker, and The Library, past the outer perimeter of the parking lot, up and over the ridge trail, along a potter's path that ran beside the still-frozen stream bed, and down through an oaky hollow into the meadow where a line was forming for The Bunker.

"Who are these people?" I said.

"It's mandatory procedure," Char said. "The whole student body is here. Try to keep your voice down. I'm working out an idea."

"You were awake when they went off."

"I'm always awake now," Char said. "I'm burning at both ends. The other day I received a shipment of speed from a friend in Iowa City. I've written ninety pages in five days."

"Your friend is a writer then."

"No. My friend is a drug dealer. He has a market there. It's a good market, too. Lots of people in Iowa City want drugs so they can write. Iowa City is famous for it."

"Ninety pages in five days must be a record. Is it any good, though?"

"What a thing to say," Char said. "Right when we're marching off to war, right when I'm churning out my first book, you have to ask if it's good. Can I just enjoy my charade, please?"

That night the darkness was total, the perfect backdrop for mourning. Everyone around us was talking in whispers, hush-hush.

"It's China," someone said.

"It's Iran," someone said.

"It's Washington," someone said.

None of us had ever been inside The Bunker. We just knew it as this awesome assemblage commissioned by former dean Harlequin Phelps in the early eighties. The Bunker was about five hundred feet in diameter, observable from the surface as a smooth concrete mound. No one knew how far underground The Bunker went, or if it connected to a larger system of tunnels, shelters, safe rooms, and escape routes. The only door was welded shut and smeared with stickers that read: NO TRESPASSING. Allegedly the walls downstairs were covered with floor-to-ceiling prints by Barbara Kruger, though there was no way to confirm if this was true.

"The Bunker is a charade, isn't it?" I said.

"The Bunker is as real as it gets," Char said. "The Bunker is the province of the purest fiction."

"We've never heard the war sirens before."

"We've been instructed on what to do when the sirens go off, but we've never actually heard them go off. Clearly this isn't a drill. Something is going on."

"The line isn't even moving, Char."

"The sirens rage across the sky like the screams of terrible children. It's the sound of horror. A bunch of little ones making a fuss about what's under the bed. Most everything else stays the same, though."

"Did you bring a spliff?" I said.

"The spliff is for the layabout," Char said. "I'm headed in the other direction. Besides, I'm just hoping we get out of line soon so

I can get back to my manuscript. I forgot to save it before we left. I'm worried about retrieval. Especially in the event of an attack."

Someone, a stranger, tapped my shoulder.

"Do you have water?" the stranger said.

"No," I said. "Do you?"

"I'm thirsty," she said.

I bent over and grabbed snow off the ground, and passed it to her in the dark.

Char leaned in then, hugging me to stay warm. I wrapped them in my arms and strained my eyes to see the stranger. Again, it was no use. The only trace of light was from The Bunker itself, still a ways out in front of us, and who knew how far. I listened to the stranger sucking on the snow, breathing faintly through her nose.

"It tastes like metal," the stranger said.

"It smells like burning plastic," I said. "What's your name? I can't see you, and I don't recognize your voice, either."

"I'm Geraldine," she said. "I'm a poet."

"We've never met, but I've heard about you from Jacobs," Char said. "I've heard you're a beautiful poet."

"Thank you for the snow," Geraldine said.

"People really hate poetry, don't they?" I said.

"They love to hate it," Geraldine said. "I think even poets hate poetry. The hatred is necessary for the love of the craft."

"How do you figure?" Char said.

"Most every other medium is self-obsessed, but poetry is self-effacing," Geraldine said. "It's a more sophisticated form of longing, which, if you take it far enough, is really just a more extreme and honest expression of love. A love without lies. Poetry destroys anything that stands in its way. And that's a good thing."

"Do you have a camera?" I said.

"I've been told we're on the brink of war," Geraldine said. "I brought a notebook and a pen. Why would I have a camera?"

The sirens went off again, this time for a full minute. We reached out for people to hold, touching whoever was there. We heard our fellow students shuffling in the night, helpless, roused from sleep, and we heard the animals over by The Barn, too, beyond the trees, bleating, crowing, mooing, quacking. A few seconds later, we registered the first gunshot, then the second, then the third. People started shouting, crying, and wailing in panic. A pack of dogs barked in the distance. There was a whooshing overhead, a screaming that seemed to bend toward where we were standing. Char and I embraced and fell to the ground, super-tight, heads to shoulders. I asked them what was happening. They just pulled me closer and sighed. The whooshing faded but quickly bounced back. It sounded like an electrical charge racing across the sky and settling above us, burrowing into our skulls. I tried to look out across the meadow, but Char held me down. I buried my head in their chest and waited. Everyone was yelling. The whooshing was constant now, much louder than before. The gunshots became a steady stream of live ammunition, aerial strafing, automatic fire. Off in the woods, there was an explosion. A second explosion rang moments later. People around us on the ground started mumbling about whatever came to mind.

"I miss my mom," someone said.

"I want to go home," another said.

"I just pissed myself twice," said a third.

The trees were engulfed in flames. The edge of the meadow looked like a burning battlefield. Students who were brave enough to stand were running around hysterically, speaking in tongues. Char covered my head with their arms as they shook, cried, and went limp. A few seconds passed, the whooshing faded, and finally the gunshots stopped. Somewhere beyond us, we heard a deafening pop, a manic rush in the darkness. Then a series of lights turned on, and it became far too bright to see. Moments later, I was able to make out the temporary fixtures ringing the meadow. We all stood there, loose on our feet now, and nearly falling over. We exchanged glances but didn't speak. Char set two little white pills in the palm of my hand. I asked what they were. They told me to just take them. I put the pills under my tongue and let them dissolve.

Geraldine came over and tapped my shoulder.

"Who's that?" she said, pointing.

Salter emerged from the trees in head-to-toe black with two cameras slung around his neck. Trailing him was Jim Arnold, wearing steampunk googles and a double-breasted suit, and Fay Huff and her partner, Maureen, an experimental ornithologist from Labrador, and together they lined up in the light and started clapping, at first softly, but soon in a concentrated roar, and Zoe strolled out from the trees and joined them in their dancing, followed by a dozen or so other professors, each of them applauding, whistling, and screaming like drunken fans at the foot of the stage, as this mopey curatorial scholar named Jarvis Hodges blew on a kazoo. His colleague, Anna Piles, threw snow into the air like paper confetti. Fay and Maureen grabbed each other and waltzed across the snow.

I leaned in and asked Char what was happening, but Char didn't hear me. I knew then, in that moment, that I wasn't really listening or hearing, either. I knew that maybe I had not been listening for quite some time now, let alone hearing, or thinking at all.

Salter lit a pale, pencil-thin cigar and took a sip from his steely flask. A spotlight turned on behind him, illuminating Grayson at the top of a tower. She held a large white megaphone in her hand. We peered up then and waited for the inevitable sermon. Grayson never spoke. She just stood there and looked down on us, surveying the field from on high, twenty or thirty feet off the ground, starring in the great human theater.

Char tapped my shoulder. It was the same type of tower used by football coaches, they said. They just thought I would like to know.

32

THE RABBI AND THE chaplain sat at the picnic table, playing back-gammon in matching suits. They shared a hoagie and a bag of pepper chips and both sipped from the same can of Diet Coke. It was the warmest day yet, the first real marker of spring. I was dangling in a nearby hammock, smoking a spliff, and watching the game unfold. The rabbi rolled the dice and made his move, causing the chaplain's round red face to tighten. The rabbi asked him, with a mouth full of hoagie, how he was getting on with God. The chaplain rolled the dice and made his move, answering the rabbi thusly:

"Well, that's just the shit of it, brother. I reckon I don't know. I'm messy for knowing. I'm talking here about the problem of bandwidth, the eternal judgments of space-time. I'm talking about where He's at and where I'm at, which are mutually exclusive positions. It's like a few months ago, after I went to Shreveport for my sister's funeral, the voices up there just went silent. The signals got crossed."

"Do you still speak to Him?" said the rabbi.

"I speak to Him, sure. I worship Him, sure. I work for Him, sure. But I can't hear His commands for diddly. That's a big change for me, and what I perceive to be my moral landscape or whatever you will. I've always heard His voice. Even when I was all sexed up and coked out in Memphis, I still always heard Him. Now I just hear static. The hum of the television. The burning of sacred books. The meaning we attribute to fire."

"Have you lost the faith?" said the rabbi.

"I can't say I lost the faith, brother. It's not that. But the conversation is slipping. I feel more alone than ever before."

The rabbi studied his options and rolled the dice and made his move. The chaplain took a sip of Diet Coke and winced at the board. Both wore black suits, starchy white shirts, and shiny, black oxford shoes. A patternless, matte-black tie hung loosely from each of their necks, like a bow. Their Take Creek–issued wool coats, also black, were carefully folded on the bench at their sides.

"That's a nice shake, brother," the chaplain said. "I damn sure admire the bravado. It's exact, to the point, stripped of all excess. That's the roll of a cutthroat seasoned player."

After the chaplain made his move, the rabbi let his head fall into the palms of his hands, intimating some vague grievance. His body locked up, and he swore in a language I didn't understand. Finally, he rolled the dice and moved his checkers, relaxing back, at last seemingly pleased with his play.

"God is a pernicious son of a bitch," he said. "I've spent over fifty years trying to come to terms with Him. I believe in what I'm doing. I love my wife. I love my children. I love my work. But God is a snaky motherfucker. Say, did you end up selling your position in JPMorgan Chase?"

The chaplain squealed.

"I just can't bring myself to do it," he said. "Banks are the bread and butter of my portfolio. They always come out on top. Plus I already got rich, so why keep pushing it? I have my farmstead in Marlonsville, my old Victorian in San Francisco, my live-work loft in the East Village, and my ranch in western Montana. The ranch is so big you can fly across it for ten minutes in a helicopter and still not make it to the neighboring property. That's all thanks to my mentor, the great preacher Lionel Davis. Ten years back Lionel died, and having no children and no living spouse, he left me his entire portfolio. I didn't know it at the time, but that squirrely shit-stomper bought ten thousand dollars of stock in a little company called Apple, right when Apple went public. Mind you, shares ran about twenty-two dollars a pop then, meaning Lionel started with roughly four hundred fifty shares. Fast forward forty years and factor in four splits. Two years ago, when I sold my position I had over twenty-five thousand shares listed at three hundred dollars a share. Do the math. I paid a lot of tax, sure. But then I bought my houses outright. Did you sort out your dividends?"

The rabbi squealed.

"I'm pulling in thirty to fifty percent yields," he said. "It should be illegal what I'm doing right now. My prized possession is a small corporation that goes by the name Polity Management of the Caribbean Basin. They probably do dirty work. But I know a squeeze when I see a squeeze. So I threw in half a mil. The next day, I threw in another half. The returns were just gross. What can I say? I like to play. I want to put it to chance. I sold off my Google, my Tesla, my Microsoft. I'm done with that tech garbage. I need a riskier venture. A couple months ago, I flew down and met with my advisor in Grand Cayman. This woman is a shark, and whip-smart on the topic of the Dutch Gilded Age. She's a scratch golfer, too, which is a quality I can't help but find fascinating. I don't play golf myself, but that's only because I don't respect the timing of the sport. There's too much idling. There isn't enough inertia. Golf requires an endless reservoir of patience. I prefer hockey. I like bullfighting. I want fast small-sided violence."

The game came to a kind of natural pause, mired in talk. I hopped out of my hammock and walked to the table and sat beside the rabbi and passed my spliff to the chaplain, whose next move was in question. The chaplain dragged on the spliff, inhaling deeply. He handed it over to the rabbi and rolled the dice. The rabbi smoked frantically, in short, manic bursts, burning the thing until it was almost embers and then reaching out and flicking it into the snow.

"These kids," said the rabbi.

"These pernicious sons of bitches," said the chaplain.

I lit two more spliffs and passed one to each of them. I stood, circling around the picnic table, frenzied and superhigh. I told them I needed advice.

"Come take a load off, brother," said the chaplain.

I went over and sat next to him. The chaplain patted my arm in solace. He reminded me that Take Creek was a safe space, or better put: an intersectional sanctuary—this being the preferred term of the rabbi, and so, too, the term that he, the chaplain, after having given the matter careful consideration, was now obliged to use in practice, mostly for the simple reason that the term did, admittedly, carry a semantic and phonetic gravitas, the likes of which had serious appeal to Take Creekers, who, in his estimation, were by and large a bunch of swooners that always buckled for the latest trend. The chaplain customarily spat a bit when he spoke. His breathing got labored and slow.

"The point of all this, brother, is that you can say or do whatever you feel like, provided it doesn't cause harm to others," the chaplain said.

"Of course," said the rabbi. "Though there are other normative statements worthy of your attention, and we hope you pursue them on your own."

"Correction," said the chaplain. "We *expect* you to pursue them on your own."

The rabbi went on.

"When we're sitting at the picnic table playing backgammon and smoking pot, the only rule is the rule of reciprocity. Are you familiar with this rule, son?"

"Love others in the way you love yourself," I said.

"Very good," said the rabbi. "Now tell us what's eating at you?"

"It's about my future," I said.

"You need to be cautious," said the chaplain. "Shit eats what shit can. Which is usually just another more virulent flavor of shit, mind you. The game of financials is a sick three-headed monster."

"The chaplain's right," said the rabbi. "If you want returns as a Take Creek grad, your parents have to be rich. Tell us, son. Are your parents rich?"

"No," I said.

"That's a shame," said the rabbi.

"An American tragedy," said the chaplain.

"A Take Creek grad without rich parents is a goner," said the rabbi.

"Yes, indeed," said the chaplain. "He'll find it hard to save in his time."

The rabbi looked at the chaplain and nodded in assent.

"The creature comforts of others will not be afforded you," he said. "And there's nothing you can do about your lot in life, either. You must endure the order of things, as it was put forth by God."

The chaplain checked his watch, an unpretentious analog quartz with a cream dial and a nutbrown leather strap. His eyes widened. His jaw went slack. He remained that way for a considerable while.

"Speaking of," he said. "It's just about time for my afternoon snoozer. I'm due for confession in The Shaker at four, and if I don't crash out for at least two hours before then, I'm liable to wring some twipster's neck. I beg your pardon, gentlemen."

He stood and tapped my cheeks with the tips of his fingers.

"Thanks for smoking me up, brother," he said. "It's damn righteous, you know, being so generous with your grass. You're peddling a rare strain there, that's for sure, if I might say so myself."

The chaplain went off for his nap, leaving the rabbi and me alone at the picnic table. We sat face to face across from one another. It looked like it was about to rain.

"The chaplain likes to talk," he said.

"It's fine," I said. "But I wasn't going to ask about investments."

"What's eating at you, son?"

"It's about my future."

"What about it?"

"I'm done in May," I said.

"You're ruminating on life after Take Creek, after the fever dream of the arts."

"I'm thinking about what comes next. I graduate. Then what?"

"No more photography," said the rabbi. "No more angles. No more depth. No more saturation. No more emulsion. No more audience. It's a known progression. I've watched the end come and go for you kids for almost two decades now. Still, every year around this time, my heart breaks again all the same."

"I guess I want guarantees," I said.

"That may prove difficult," he said.

"Difficult how?"

"Impossible is probably a better word."

"Why can't you give me assurances?"

"Against what, son?"

"Against burning mediocrity. And disappointment. And sadness. And zero hope. And slow dusty death."

"God is infinite, but also transcendent," said the rabbi. "His law is of another language and unintelligible to mere mortals. This is His way. So what, though? Get over it and move on. Take it lightly. You sound like a young narcissistic psychopath right now, which, by the way, surprises me. It's usually the rich kids who have the bigger conniptions. Why you? What happened?"

"Does it get easier, rabbi?"

"No," he said. "It's going to get much harder. Have you met with the Options Counselor?"

"I've been putting it off," I said.

The rabbi glanced, shaking his head.

"The numbers are astronomical, son. It's totally mad. A kind of foible. Nevertheless, you need to speak with someone so you can learn to live with your choices. That's the truth of the thing. This isn't God's fault. It's yours. You chose to come here. You assumed the responsibility. Now you have to face the tender. I'm not saying that it's just. But it's how the system functions. You'll have to vote in new politicians who care about your plight, and then they'll have to figure out how to deal with it, all the while ensuring that they don't get bought out by the banks and the friends of the banks along the way, which seems unlikely, but certainly not impossible, especially if you factor in the possibility of all-out revolution, but who knows? Not me, son. That, too, seems like a long shot right now. Plus the revolutionaries tend to become tyrants. The cycle has been playing out for millennia. Still we keep spinning the luxuriant wheel. With every spin we hope to get it a little bit better."

"You believe that history is on repeat. Is that right, rabbi."

"Of course not. It's a metaphor."

"But where's the wheel then?"

"I guess you need to find it. Until you do, you'll have to pray, or at least try. Tell me, son. Are you a Jew?"

"No."

"Are you a believer?"

"No."

"Then who do you pray to?"

"I don't."

"That's a shame."

The rabbi passed me what was left of his hoagie. I took a bite, not realizing how hungry I was. He packed up the backgammon board and watched me while I chewed, slowly, super-high. I could have stayed there for hours talking through the heavy parts, but the rabbi needed to be going. He wished me luck and told me to check back in with him whenever I could, and I said I would. I tugged at his sleeve as he stood and grabbed his coat. He turned around and looked down at me.

"Rabbi, can I ask you one last question?"

"Anything you need, son."

"Is there a rogue sect in Haifa connected to Mossad?" I said.

The rabbi just burst out laughing.

I walked back to The Barracks and tried to take a nap, but I couldn't sleep, and time was just spinning. I lay there for a while longer in the darkness. Then I went out looking for Manning. I banged on the door to his studio and called his phone. I texted. I emailed. I called again. I banged more. He didn't answer. The light was on at the window, and the shades had all been drawn. I could hear music coming from inside the room, also voices, muffled and faint. The light went out. The music got louder. I sat on the concrete stoop and put my ear to the door, craning my neck, convinced I heard her voice. It was the last song off Moniker's first record, I knew, a wry worker's ballad, which had been recorded over ten years ago, but would forever be Jersey's favorite.

33

(HANNA AND I WERE taking an experimental sprint seminar on The Nature of Sudden Events. It was taught by a wormy, underdressed visiting professor named Megan Mendelson, who insisted we call her Meg. The course was three weeks long, consisting of six twenty-minute sessions. Enrollment was limited to two students per section. There was no required reading or writing, and ours was the only section of its kind. We met on Monday and Tuesday nights just before nine in a recently requisitioned building near The Farley Gardens, a damp poorly lit room where Meg set up chairs and a table with two clip-on lapel microphones to record our various exchanges. Tonight was our fourth session, but Hanna and I still had no idea what we were doing.)

HANNA

There's a low pressure system building off Kamchatka.
An earthquake in Lombok opened a sinkhole a half mile wide.

ME

The Senior Spokesperson for the Italian Coast Guard

confirmed that today it had found the remains of an Algerian ship in the Strait of Sicily. The ship, which was reported missing Friday, was believed to be carrying approximately five hundred migrants from Libya to Italy, all of whom perished at sea.

HANNA

A police officer in Pine Bluff, Arkansas shot a ten-year-old girl when she stopped them to ask for directions. A police officer in Oakland, California accidentally shot and killed a man for not paying a parking meter after the officer mistook his Glock for his Taser.

MEG

Later that day, a thirty-two-year-old woman froze to death in Miles City, Montana, just as the Dow Jones hit an all-time high.

(Meg paced around the table and listened to our exchange on large studio headphones. She fixed her sallow gaze on Hanna and jotted notes on a legal yellow pad with a red marker. Meg had this magnetic spiky hair, unshorn and wiry, in medium brown. She was tall and angular, without a trace of fat or muscle. Her sweatpants and sweatshirt were two sizes too big, falling to the floor at her heels. Hanna peered over at me, gently rolling her eyes. She looked more than a little confused.)

ME

This is weird, Meg. We're just rambling about the news, tit for tat, trading small zingers about whatever we happen to be absorbing. Much of what I've said isn't true at all. I'm making it up.

HANNA

Me, too.

MEG

The entire point of the exercise is to riff back and forth.
The nature of events is the same, to ebb and flow. An
event is anything that's relevant to you.

ME

You really mean anything?

MEG

It's an experimental sprint seminar. We're exploring embodied psychosocial cognition. Everything is
connected. Every point has relevance in the emergent
status of the event, provided the event emerges at all. A
firestorm. A coup d'etat. A home-cooked meal. A bout
of strep throat. Everything has purchase.

HANNA

Even if it's not true?

MEG

Sure. Why not? Talk about whatever you want. Would
either of you like a glass of water before we go on?"

HANNA

No.

ME

No.

MEG

Thank goodness. I forgot my water bottle in my office, and this old building barely has power, let alone working pipes. Hanna, please continue.

HANNA

A highly infectious game is spreading across campus.

ME

Last week, Amazon sold out of a particular brand of helmets and face masks. Peter Delacroix immediately went into hiding.

HANNA

Zoe gave an impromptu talkback at which she threw green olives at the audience, spat on the stage, and said that everyone there was a loping and sappy dog.

ME

The next day, an iceberg the size of Philadelphia broke off Antarctica. The day after that, a storm in Bangladesh killed more than two-hundred thousand people, displacing millions from their homes.

(Meg idled by the door for a time. She was working at something on the side of her mouth. It looked like she was chewing the inside of her cheek, using her fist to stretch it out. She walked back to the table and sat and rested her knees upon the floor. Hanna was doing her best not to laugh, though she looked more lost than before. When Meg finally raised her eyes, her lips quivered and turned purple. I picked back up with the weather.)

ME

It was unseasonably warm here at the time, and it's stayed unseasonably warm for weeks. The snow melted in a matter of days, flooding farms down the valley and stranding dozens of cows in a sunken bog. Every night now, our sunsets burn the color of outrage, scarred by oblong soupy clouds.

HANNA

The power went out for the fourth time this year, so we lit candles in old cans of olive oil.

ME

It was perfect. But then we got word that Mary Frankel was found dead in Aleppo, shot twice in the back of the head. Salter wrote her obituary, which was first published in *The New York Times*, and then translated into fifty-eight languages and syndicated around the world.

HANNA

Two days later, Todd Mackintosh and Jasmine Fincher got engaged and invited everyone for celebratory coffee and donuts in The Chow Hall.

ME

I said I was too busy to go.

HANNA

There's a bomb cyclone building off the coast of California. An earthquake in Chile caused an avalanche, and soon after, a landslide destroyed the copper mining village of El Tigre and took the lives of every last breathing soul who lived there.

ME

Everything tastes salty to me right now. Everything is granular.

HANNA

Meanwhile, Take Creek is suddenly rife with blooming foliage, in the warmest spring on record. The wisteria. The roses. The tulips. The lilacs. The hydrangeas. Everything is blowing the mold and eking its way to the light. The air is almost adhesive, smelling of fresh honey. Hay fever is raging. I have a constant itch in my throat. Not to mention, all this purplered acne breaking out like a blistering hive across my face.

ME

I've been following him, it's true. I'm not supposed to talk about it, but I installed cameras all over campus and I've been watching everything he does. Manning is still holed up in his studio. Franny is going there every day to visit him, often two or three times a day. Most days, they seem to just sit there and talk, but occasionally they step out of the frame, and I don't have a clue what the two of them are doing.

HANNA

Yesterday morning, the Wild Dogs issued a missive, demanding respect and money for the upcoming season. Some of us are referring to them as a cult, others just a team. When you think about it, though, the distinction between the two terms isn't all that clear to begin with.

ME

My father finally stopped calling. Then my mother wrote me a letter, begging me to call. My brother sent me an email and asked me to be reasonable. He attached two recent photographs of him and Tamela: one at a line dance in Denton; one at a ribbon-cutting ceremony for his newest Subway franchise.

HANNA

A few hours ago, Jacobs posted a picture on Instagram from the Seychelles, where she donned a string bikini and one of those sunhats made out of fake straw. The caption read: SABBATICAL OR BUST. I couldn't keep it in.

(Meg came out of the dark corner into the light and stepped nearer
to the table. She looked excited. She was sweating profusely. She
patted Hanna's back, then mine. She set her legal pad and marker
on the table and started dancing around the room.)

HANNA

What are you doing?

MEG

I'm skanking.

ME

It looks like you're running in place, Meg.

MEG

That's the point. Say, can you show me that recent
post? I just have to see it to believe it. Everyone tells me
Jacobs used to have a swastika tattooed above her left
breast. Did either of you happen to notice? Now it's
covered up with a mandala, but apparently if you look
closely enough you can still see it. It's still there, pitching
out faintly through the circle.

34

Now, one warm Sunday evening, just after Jersey dyed his hair blonde and his eyebrows black, I was sitting in the basement again, alone at the computer, under the lamp, going through footage from the cameras. I wasn't looking for anything specific, or if I was looking for something I didn't know what it was, or where I might find it, or how I might see it, if at all, in this light. Nor was I thinking through the video. I was simply watching it, simply there: the following body in the room.

Salter said film was the ultimate terror.

Salter said film had supplanted lived experience and there was nothing left to do save shoot.

Cinema was built on the photograph, but cinema was forever running away from itself, shifting before our eyes, dreadful, lifelike, banal. A photograph on the other hand could break the flow and hold it, retaining a trace of what was, once upon a time, an undeniable certainty. It was the moment that kept going, always hinting toward death and disappearance, and ultimately, defeat.

Tonight I watched Franny as she strolled around Manning's room, smoking a spliff while wearing his underwear. She stood above him. He sprawled out naked on the floor and shivered and shook and mumbled. I watched them play back and forth like that for hours, until very late at night. Manning poured endless cups of tea. Franny touched him and her body seemed to buckle, softly tugging at his back and hips with her hands. The world out there was growing fainter. Its tempo exceeded my grasp. But I would let the sensations trickle in and seek their own level. Franny was gone to me now. I knew this much to be true. Yet I somehow felt free watching her with Manning, watching them move together on camera. I put on Muzak and cranked up the volume, kicking back in the chair and stretching out.

These days, Salter was gone well over half the time, on assignment in yet another undisclosed location, for yet another undisclosed number of days. I had printed five variations of the snow photograph that were ready for his review. I was pleased with the results, though I had no idea if Salter would agree. Graduation loomed. There was yellow police tape draped across the door to his office, and hanging from a nail, a laminated sign that read: KEEP OUT. BIOHAZARD. His voice was everywhere, humming in my ear, telling me which objects were real and which were imagined.

Now, one warm Sunday evening, just after Jersey dyed his hair blonde and his eyebrows black, and just after Char finished their novel and called it *Cha* and that was that, I sat in a basement way upstate, buried in the pines, acting the part of the voyeur. I had held out hope for months, but that was all gone now, flowing away like hot rain. This assignment, this circumstance, this looming final project, maybe even Take Creek itself—all of it suddenly felt like a farce. I had grown tired of being strung along, baying like a dog on a leash. I knew I needed to graduate, and I would do whatever it took, but when it was done, that would be the end for me, the absolute, no looking back, the point where I finally broke form. Because if the following actually changed you, if it actually did realign your neurons or something otherwise more radical, then Salter was wrong. This wasn't the following. This was just a sickness in the human heart. This was his pathology curled up like a worm in a dark corner of the room. I turned off the lamp and switched on the overhead light. I deactivated the cameras and froze access to the account by changing the username and password. Then I shut down the computer, grabbed my camera, and went out walking into the still black night.

These days Gregor was channeling an avant-garde South Coaster named Blanch. Blanch lived in a single-room occupancy hotel and was showing at a Midtown gallery in Atlanta. She tied cordage into large-scale knots and shot them in various locations. Filthy sidewalks. Bathtubs. Tree wells. Tire stacks. Roadside rest areas. Sandy embankments. Stained hospital beds. Swampy bogs. There were hundreds in the series, knots of cordage in the most random, human settings. Blanch enlarged the images, but just barely. They were ten-by-ten prints, roughly the size of a vinyl record. The images presented like high-gloss flashes, which looked even glossier when they hung on a wall, like painted toys of plastic frames.

Blanch said the object of concern was always temporality. She didn't give a damn if anyone liked that, or understood what it meant.

Tonight, the half-moon splayed its creamy light across the trees. A warm wind welled, slight and songful from the west. Take Creek faded to shadows and became unrecognizable. I shot it all for the last time on my Nikon D5 in a custom function called *Frogfeet* and laughed.

Aspersions.

Cataracts.

Renderings of forms.

Tomorrow, I would go back to shooting infrared color film like Mary Frankel. Tomorrow, I would go somewhere new, and when I got there, I would reposition the background so it stood out more intensely, in the shape of a broken box. I closed my eyes and rolled a spliff with one hand as I crossed The Quad. The clouds blew in, mean and low, swirling like oil in water over the treetops and hills. I zipped up my jacket and pulled on my hood, resolved to put one foot in front of the other, deliberate and warm—that would be the way now—just as I had known from the beginning.

35

CHAR PLOWED DOWN THE back stairs and burst into the reading room in their gold polka-dot pajamas. They were lightheaded, by way of running, looking flushed, and excited more than a little. I gazed up from my book—a tome on state terrorism during the Great Wars—and winced. Traces of the day's last light flared through two rectangular windows on the adjacent wall. On the table a half-full can of sugar-free cola fizzed away in wanting. I took a long, dramatic sip and went all stargazer to get their attention.

"I'm presuming this has something to do with the Wild Dogs," I said.

"The what?" Char said.

I threw up my hands in disbelief.

"The football team," I said. "It's like an infection spreading across campus. People are losing interest in art. I fear we're becoming one of those schools where people beat drums and grunt like idiots. Are you serious you don't know about the Wild Dogs? Just come out with it already, would you?"

"An agent in New York picked up *Cha*," Char said. "It's finally happening for me. I might soon be a published novelist."

I leapt up and howled. I hugged Char and pulled them down to the floor, putting my hands on their cheeks and kissing their nose.

"This is the best news I've ever heard," I said. "I'm so happy for you. I'm so proud of you. My dear pal Char is going out into the world. And there's nothing anyone can do to stop them."

"Thanks," Char said. "I just got the email. I ran all over campus looking for you. I saw Salter in The Quad. He said if you knew what was good for you, you should check the reading room."

"He's back then?" I said.

"It would seem so," they said. "He was carrying a weird old boxy camera and wearing a hazmat suit."

"He finally emailed the other day and said I had to read this book. It's really long. But the implications are intense. The author is a French woman named Marie Trevisse. She writes about war and catastrophe as the perfect opportunity to reinvent the world. There's margin in mystery, she says."

"It seems like we could read that statement on other levels, too," Char said.

"The implications are intense either way," I said.

"It looks like Salter is losing weight," Char said. "I wonder if we should be worried. Not that he'd listen to us anyway. I'm just calling it out."

"What comes next?" I said.

"The agent tries to find a publisher," Char said. "It could be a dead end."

"Don't say that."

"Your guess is as good as mine. But you're right. It's a major first step."

"First step?" I said, incredulous. "I think you mean one-thou-sand-fifty-first step. Lots of people, probably all people, have novels inside of them. Writing the thing is hard enough. Let alone submitting it. Let alone getting an agent. You truly are a boxer."

"Thanks," Char said, blushing.

"Have you spoken to Jacobs?"

"I can't wait to write her and tell her what's happening to me. I wish I could see the look on her tanned face when she hears that my work was accepted by a big Midtown agent. I hope her bungalow shakes on its laurels."

"When do we celebrate?"

"Soon," Char said. "I have to build a diorama for a seminar on modality. It's due tomorrow and I haven't even started yet. I'm way behind on all my assignments because of *Cha*. It's kind of daunting to even think about how I'm going to catch up."

"Well, soon then," I said, to which Char assented with a nod and a wave.

Later that night, Jersey woke me in one of his typical furies. I had no idea what time it was. There was a large pool of drool on the pillow, and my underwear and socks were all missing. Jersey wore latex gloves. His face had been blotted with sunscreen under his eyes and along his jawline. I could smell the stuff as he leaned over to ask if I was conscious.

"You woke me from a volcano dream," I said. "I was climbing the volcano but there was no one else there. It was just me."

"Where was the volcano?" he said.

"I'm not sure. It was so hot. The air was piping hot and gross. The landscape kept changing as I ascended. The trees smelled like rotting corpses. There were banana trees, coffee trees, cacao trees, marijuana plants, clove trees, and then I was in a forest full of tufty ferns, following a stream up a steep muddy trail. Soon there were no trees left, and I was walking through a vacant land of rocks and scree. There was an observatory at the edge of a cliff. Two scientists in white lab coats waved at me from a distance. I kept going. I wasn't worried about food or water. Should I have been worried about food or water?"

"We have a situation," Jersey said. "And it requires your full cooperation."

"I'm listening," I said. "But I'm not queueing up for another war drill."

Jersey took a deep breath, gathering himself in a way that seemed more serious than it actually was.

"It's imperative that we get to nature right now. Your dream is no mistake. We need to absorb the view from up there. Then we need to get to the coast. It's imperative that we dive down and see the wreck. Do you understand what I'm telling you?"

"No," I said. "You sound crazy right now."

"Why are you being so fucking stupid?" he said.

"Aren't we already deep in nature here?" I said.

"You're losing your mind. That's the dumbest question you've asked me in years. This is important, so listen up. This is maybe the most important thing we've ever faced. At least up until now. At this point in our lives."

I tried to calm Jersey down. He wouldn't listen, though. He pinned me to the bed, put his gloved hand over my mouth, and told me to shut up or else. And shut up I quickly did.

"I'll talk to Holly about borrowing a truck from her dad and taking us into nature sometime soon," he said.

"Who's Holly?"

Jersey shooed me off.

"A climbing friend," he said. "Her dad has this obscenely large white truck. It could ford a river in optimal conditions. I'll be in touch about a plan. Until then, don't muck it up. Not a word about this to anyone."

"Who would I tell? I don't even have a girlfriend anymore," I said.

"I heard about that," he said, patting my head.

"You heard how?"

"I've had suspicions for a while, but earlier tonight, I saw them strolling arm in arm through The Farley Gardens. I'm sorry for you. It really is such a doozy."

"You're saying Manning is out in the world now? You're saying he's left his cloister and come to join us townsfolk?"

"I'm afraid it's true." Jersey said.

"What did you do?" I said.

Jersey paused and pretended to stroke the beard he didn't have.

His face tightened like he was mining a question of higher math or astrophysics.

"What do you think I did?" he said. "I flipped them the bird. I lit a medium fire with broken branches on the ground at my feet. I flipped them the bird again and poured a gallon of white gas on the fire. Then I left. I walked away."

I smiled. Jersey started laughing. Maybe he had a point there, or something.

36

I COULDN'T SAY HOW it all got started. I couldn't give the exact moment or reason why. But that night on the bus, it was like something just turned over inside me, and I knew I wasn't the same as before. From Marlonsville, we rode north up Highway 95 to Oak Junction, merging onto the Upstate Superhighway in a surge of hot white light. The air conditioners and TVs were all broken. The toilet was out of order. The towns were marked by signs that raced past the window in caustic, dream-like flashes.

Brokersville. Hamtown. Crawford. Miller's Landing.

The world cauterized at night.

The world hemmed in.

My seatmate spoke to herself in a brutal mumble the whole way there. Her name was Lucky Michelle, and she was coming home from Philadelphia. She wore a loose gauze bandage over the sleeve of her jean jacket. She stuffed Kleenex in both ears as she wept. Somehow I managed to sleep a little on the journey, reaching Commerce City at first light the following morning, exhausted and sour, short of breath, with my backpack in my lap and two large bags of stale potato chips for dinner, both Nacho Cheese, long gone, the wrappers crumpled into wads, the crumbs everywhere, the piles in tatters all over the seats.

I was standing on the curb outside the station when Lucky Michelle came up from behind me.

"What happened?" she said.

"What do you mean?" I said.

"Is everybody dead?" she said.

I looked at her and thought of my brother. Sometimes there was just nothing else left to say to a person.

"You want to get a drink somewhere?" she said.

"Not exactly," I said.

"Well, you want to get a ride to the spot? You want to go smoke some opium with my ex-husband and his kid brother?"

Lucky Michelle followed me inside to the bathroom, and when I walked back out, she was gone.

It was the year everyone around me seemed to be leaving, pushing off. There were so many different people living through my life at any given time. Not that long ago, they were all still there. The next time I checked, it seemed half of them had fled. Somebody once told me to expect that, to expect all of them leaving at some point, and to get used to it now because it only got worse.

I had come to Commerce City to see a show, a one-night-only event at a small gallery called Z Wall. The show would feature new work by Devlin, an offbeat photographer who shot for Magnum, one of my favorites of all time. I had dreamed of shooting just like Devlin, someday, down the line.

Dusky haunts, secret faces, the cities of the plain in light and shadow.

These, too, I hoped to one day catalogue, shooting at Devlin's side.

I walked the streets of Commerce City all morning, through neighborhoods with boarded-up storefronts and abandoned factories. The houses I passed were old and stately, but most sat vacant or had been torn down altogether. The adjacent lots looked like overgrown pastures, brimming with weeds, knee-high sunflowers, wild dahlias, giant tufts of yellowgreen grass. It was as if the land itself had finally overcome the city, staking some ancient claim and assuming its rightful place.

I didn't know where I was going. I was just walking, moving in distended circles, taking photographs of whatever was there.

A fire burned in a barrel down a back alley.

People kept waving at me.

The air smelled like hot prairie rain.

I found a café on a wide empty street. The café was L-shaped, a small spot on the corner, a counter joint known as Hazel's. The windows faced the street. This was a quiet place with only a few passing cars. Music played softly from speakers mounted on the wall above the till, an old bop record spinning on a turntable. I ordered a cup of coffee and a tuna sandwich and asked the server what I should see while I was in town.

The woman tapped her fingers on the counter, head cocked, looking up. She had green eyes and a sharp-jawed face framed by long, radiant curls. She wore a teal apron. A thin gold ring was pierced through her septum.

"That depends on what you're looking for," she said.

"I'm not sure," I said. "I'm here for a show tonight, but I have the entire day to spare. I'm open to just about anything."

"Where are you from?" she said.

"I was born in Houston," I said. "What about you?"

"I was born in Trinidad," she said. "But I've lived in Commerce City since I was four, except for a six-year stint in New York. The city wasn't for me. My name's Hazel. This is my place. What's the show?"

"I'm about to graduate from college with a degree in photography," I said. "And one of my favorite photographers is showing new work here tonight. Her name's Devlin. I came to see her. I have to see her."

"I totally forgot," Hazel said, shaking her head. "I'm glad you stopped by. I promised her I'd go."

"You know Devlin?" I said.

"My younger brother is Devlin's best friend. She was at my wedding. We grew up together. Of course I know Devlin."

A silver-eyed postman walked into the café. Hazel emerged from behind the counter and hugged him, pinching his cheeks. She poured him a large coffee and waved him off when he asked how much.

"I got this one," she said. "Give Louise and your girls a squeeze for me."

When the postman left, Hazel turned to me as if in study, idling among the tables.

"You seriously came all this way for Devlin's show?" she said.

I said yes.

I told her about the overnight bus ride and that I was sorry if I smelled, was in bad shape, or looked unseemly, so to speak.

"It's called the Hound," she said. "It's always like that. If it weren't like that, you wouldn't be in America now, would you?"

I laughed, sipped my coffee, waited.

"I'll tell you what," she said. "My relief gets here in about an hour. How about I show you around this afternoon."

"Really?" I said.

"Sure. Why not?"

"I don't know what to say."

"Just say okay. It's no big deal. I've got nothing to do, and it sounds fun to play tourist for a change. Besides, this city has more stories than most."

A woman wearing hospital scrubs walked into the café, trailed by two pale freckled boys, identical twins, maybe seven or eight years old, both beaming. Next came a group of construction workers, talking softly in Spanish, all carrying hard hats at their sides. Another group walked in moments later. And soon after, another. A cribbage club. A family of five. Four women. A rabbi and an imam. Two women. A motorcycle gang. A crew of house painters. A team of social workers. A group of students discussing a book called *Hopscotch*. Before long, the café was full, overwhelmed by the din of the gathered. People kept filing in off the street, content just to stand there and wait, chasing the promise known only to crowds.

We drove past a long stretch of row homes on a narrow tree-lined street where Hazel had lived for years with her husband and son. We circled the neighborhoods along the river, across downtown, into the railyards, and Hazel called out each place by name as we passed. She showed me where the first factory was erected in the early 1800s, a former mill at Camden, the site of a ruthless attack on the Seneca, whose land had been stolen for pennies and swamp fever. The mill quickly prospered, and other mills soon followed suit, especially once the Trans-Upstate Canal was completed in the early nineteenth century, and even more so when the railroad arrived decades later, connecting Commerce City to other markets. The city grew hand over fist during these years. The logging industry boomed, milling lumber that built many of the great Northern cities. Flour mills sprouted on the riverfront. Then came seed companies and nurseries. During the Civil War, the city was a hub for abolitionists and a noted stop on the Underground Railroad. Freed slaves moved to Commerce City by the thousands. It turned out that women's suffrage was pretty much born here too. In the late nineteenth and early twenti-eth centuries the city became home to many of the country's most powerful companies. Lenses. Film. Telegraphs. Prepared food. Garments. Shoes. Machines. Automobiles. Production kept accel-erating during wartime, people kept arriving, but after the war, that all slowed. White flight changed the city forever. The population declined, the economy collapsed, and poverty became the norm, especially for the poor black and brown residents who remained. Police violence reached new levels. Racism existed wherever you looked. In the decades to come, Commerce City grew bleaker in every possible way. Factories closed. Schools were boarded up. Hospitals took on the face of empty tenements. Parks were laid fallow. Roads cracked, fell to pieces, sunk. Most of the city was unlit. The electricity turned on and off without notice. Life carried on, Hazel said, but there was no work, no education, no public services, no functioning utilities. And eventually the city filed for bankruptcy. What had once been one of the most profitable cities in the entire country, a city that lined the pockets of many early industrialists and corporate robber barons, was now on its knees, totally tapped. The last twenty years had shown signs of promise and hope, Hazel said, but there was a long way to go.

"It takes a lot of love and family," she said, "Which is exactly what we do every day at the café. Even though the population is only thirty percent of what it was after World War Two, more than half of the city's residents were born abroad. Somalis. Syrians. Yemenis. Mexicans. Salvadoreans. Ukrainians. Poles. Kazaks. Punjabis. Indonesians. Not to mention Trinidadians. This city has the largest Trinidadian community in the country. They keep coming and we keep saying, *let them in, we'll take care of you.* That's what Commercials do. It's what we call ourselves. What we've been called. For hundreds of years, in fact. Commercials. Isn't that funny?" she said.

We rode on, both laughing.

The sun sagged into a grayblue veil.

We stopped for a snack at Mary Franks, a roadside attraction where the house special was the Commercial Coney, a broiled all-beef hot dog served on a steamed bun and topped with diced white onions, mustard, cheddar cheese, hot sauce, and dill relish. The line stretched halfway to the corner.

"What are you going to do when you graduate?" Hazel said, chewing on her Coney and watching me chew mine.

"This is a really good hot dog," I said.

We were laughing again, reaching for our drinks. I was catching my breath before going on.

"I have no idea what I'm doing," I said. "I just want to shoot what I feel like shooting."

Hazel sat across the booth and listened intently, though she gave me no assurances or indications for how to proceed.

"What's Take Creek like?" she said.

"It's a strange place," I said. "Very small. Really intense. There's a lot of clout and famous faculty. My mentor's a photographer named Salter, and he's kind of going nuts. Lately it's gotten even more out of hand. We have this violent football team running around campus day and night, terrorizing anyone who stands in its way."

"That sounds expensive."

"You can't imagine," I said. "I'll be in the hole with the banks until I die."

We drove south across the canal, past the café, past the stadium and the run-down train station, and then down a bumpy road abutting the river. Hazel parked in front of an unmarked ware-house. I followed her to the door, and she knocked. The door opened to a tall grinning woman with bleached hair, shoul-der-length, wearing wire-rimmed glasses and a dark blue dress, her bare feet hot white on the pavement.

It was Devlin Hancock.

Hazel and Devlin hugged and kissed each other on the cheek. It was the type of embrace reserved only for close family and the dearest of friends, a drawn out and cathartic gesture, deeply human but rare to see. Hazel told Devlin she met a young photographer who had come to Commerce City for tonight's show. I could barely speak. I shook Devlin's hand and told her what an honor.

"That's really sweet of you," Devlin said. "Please, come inside."

Hazel touched Devlin's shoulder.

"I'm going to wait by the car," she said to me.

I nodded.

"Take as long as you need," she added. "I'm sure you two have a lot to talk about."

I cupped my hands, for absolutely no reason, and then followed Devlin into her studio and warehouse. The space was massive, bright and open and full of colorful rugs and assorted furniture, a space broken into discrete areas, with shelves weighed down by books and cameras, with photographs hanging everywhere on the walls. Soft light rained down from the slatted dormers and checkered casements overhead. There were metal fixtures dangling from the ceiling, none of which were anything alike. Devlin brewed a pot of tea and offered me a cigarette. We went and sat on a curved maroon sofa, the center of the space she dubbed The Parlor.

"The Parlor is my special spot," Devlin said. "It's where I hide out from the fold."

"I can't believe I'm sitting here with you," I said.

"Why is that?"

"I took the overnight bus all the way from Marlonsville. I came here to see your work. I met Hazel this morning at the café. She's been really good to me. She showed me around the city and told me stories. Now I'm here. I don't believe it. This can't be real."

Devlin set her mug on the table, then she grabbed a camera and asked if she could take my picture.

"I shoot everyone that comes over," she said. "House policy."

I settled deeper into the sofa and looked at the lens. Devlin raised the viewfinder to her eye and focused, a soft gaze, her subject caught in sudden repose.

"So you're a photographer," she said.

"I am."

"That's wonderful," she said. "Do you have any work on hand?"

I opened a recent portfolio on my laptop, a selection of work that spanned years of context and material. Devlin scrolled through the shots frame by frame, with deliberate presence, taking her time. She didn't pose the usual questions or seek explanation in the work, and she never once asked about my goals, or where I went to school, or how long I had been shooting, or why I got into shooting in the first place. When she finished, she went to the stove and lit a cigarette at one of the burners.

"Where are you headed?" she said, turning around.

"I don't know."

"Give me a hint."

"I'm making it up as I go."

"I think there's probably more than that."

Devlin walked back to The Parlor and sat beside me, smoking.

"These photographs are impressive," she said. "Your style has real bandwidth. The subject matter is complex and varied, and for someone your age, the command of the equipment is just wild. When you're ready, you can do whatever you want with this work. But frankly, you don't have to do anything. Many of the best artists I know do the work for themselves and themselves alone. That's a beautiful craft in its own right, and chock-full of honor, too. But I'd encourage you to carry the process into the next stages of your life, in whatever form that takes. Why am I saying this? What's the point? These are fair questions. Because who really knows? I still ask myself the same things every day. And I'm almost fifty. I've been at this for a long time. That doesn't mean I have the answers or that I know what's best for you. I just think you should keep at it, is all."

"Salter says the same."

"Salter?"

"He's my professor at Take Creek."

"Jimmy Salter," she said, looking off. "He was a good photographer at one point, maybe even a great one. But nowadays, he's just a total debaser."

"Salter says I need to keep grinding," I said.

"Grinding?" Devlin said.

"Salter says that's what Take Creek does. It teaches you how to grind. He says I need to grind like no one's ever grinded before, and that I can't stop, either, especially if I want to shoot for Magnum."

"That's gross," Devlin said. "You should thank the old creep for what he's done for you. But then you should move on. You have a lot of work to explore here, and much more to come. I know you'll find a home somewhere for these shots, but it's going to take patience. I would like to help you in whatever way I can."

Devlin wrote her phone number and email address on a piece of scrap paper, wide-rule, yellow legal. She stood up and handed it to me.

"I really appreciate you taking the time," I said.

"This is what we do," she said. "We help each other out. I didn't get to where I am today without help. Just stop using that word *grinding*, okay? You sound like a spoilsport. And also a really gross guy. Just because your world right now is teeming with angsty kids in kimonos and berets, and they're all blabbing about some new French theory but not doing anything themselves, that doesn't mean you have to do the same thing as them. It has to be different for you, if you choose this life. Your commitments have to be clearer. Do you really want to be an artist?"

I said yes.

"Then you need to cut out all the mental hopscotch. You need to be accurate, compassionate, and exacting. This isn't a grind. It's an act of love."

That night, after the show, I took the bus home by way of Greenfern, Coopersville, Cold River, Franklin's Pass. Even though my connection in Elmsborough was delayed more than two hours, I still made it back to Take Creek just before lunch. When I walked into The Chow Hall, the scent of a salty, old-world stew lofted in the air, pork or beef or mutton—who among us knew which? I ladled two large servings into compostable to-go containers and went outside to eat on the grass.

The landscape kept changing, racing away from me. Clouds of yellow pollen blew off the trees and settled at my feet like toxic dust. I sat quietly under a giant maple tree and regarded the players as they passed. The Wild Dogs, now numbering more than fifty, were chanting hymns in Ancient Greek, running intervals in matching gas masks.

37

I WENT TO OFFICE hours to talk about my progress.

"Now there's a bespoke young shooter if I ever saw one."

"I got a haircut. I shaved. I'm taking a break from smoking."

"Self-betterment is an illusory calling. I'd be careful how far you take the notion. Me myself, I've just returned from western China. I flew from Urumqi, to Beijing, to San Francisco, to Chicago, to Lakeport, to here. It was a helluva slog. I'm finally sleeping normal. My mentals are once again sharp. I'm ready to talk story. Sorry it took me so long to get back to your emails. My word, were there a lot of those!

"What were you shooting in China?"

"It's a sensitive issue. I signed a non-disclosure agreement with the legal team. I'm under contract. I wish I could say more about the nature of the project, but that's not possible. Still we keep meeting like this, don't we, kid?"

"We do. But not for much longer. The end is close. I'm beginning to see it happening all around us."

"Graduation. From the late Middle English. The crux of which should remind you that we live in a world of transgressions and borrowings and theft. Have you had a chance to read Marie Trevisse yet? I'm eager to hear your impressions."

"I'm about three quarters of the way through. It's a difficult book, but I've learned a lot about opportunity in crisis."

"Hot dog. That's the steeplechaser in you talking. Her book makes some hearty leaps, but it's necessary for any course of study. I reread it every two years to stay apace. Moving forward it seems we have two major orders of business today. Let's start with the first, the following. I want conclusive data out of you, and I wanted it yesteryear. What can you tell me about Manning?"

"It's a lot. It makes me squeamish just thinking about it."

"Do I look fazed to you, kid? Do I appear to you in this moment as a man that's afraid of his own lonesome death?"

"You look the same as always, only now you're wearing head-to-toe denim, growing out a beard, sporting a fuzzy orange hunting cap."

"That's beside the point. Tell me what the sap wants."

"It seems Manning is working for a rogue group that's connected to Mossad."

"Israelis?"

"Right."

"Hmmm."

"I beg your pardon."

"I'm thinking, kid. If there are Israelis, there are usually Americans."

"I suspect so."

"US Guv strikes again. Everywhere I go, I learn something new. That much is certain."

"Manning's affiliated with larger, more nefarious global currents. I haven't been able to uncover the intention of his work, though."

"I need to just sit with this for a sec and sort out my mentals. I support divestment, sure. But I don't have a lick against the Israelis. I've visited their country many times. It's a staggeringly beautiful land, though I think they should share it and stop trying to make it bigger. What does Mossad want with me?"

"I don't know exactly. But it's all quite worrisome. I fear for your safety. Someone is plotting something against you."

"Ouch. That hurts bad. Real bad. That there is more ensconcing than a pile of day-old deershit being thrown into the stoking fire. What curious souls. What sick debasements. I don't know where to begin. But I'm definitely wary all of a sudden. That said, it's always been a secret wish of mine to harbor grave interests on a worldwide scale. I'm a misplaced rook in the great game of empire. And those suckers picked the wrong rook to mess with. I'll call Jim and let him know as soon as you leave. He needs to hear what's brewing. He's my best damn friend. The only other person I rightly trust. The bard of the desert arroyo. A human being of true mentionable honor. Are we still tracking that clumpy toad Manning on those itty bitty cameras I sent to you?"

"That's just it. Someone backchanneled us while you were gone. I'm no longer able to log in to the system. It's frozen. They changed the username and the password. The Nodes are dead, too. Or if they're still alive, someone else is watching them. Either way it isn't us. Bad news, I think, maybe."

"Methinks the same, kid. Well said. What should I do, do you think?"

"You're asking me what you should do?"

"Don't make me ask again."

"This is totally beyond me. I have no clue how to answer that question."

"Just toss out ideas. If I think they're stupid, I'll let you know."

"You could talk to the higher-ups."

"Negative."

"You could—"

"The higher-ups don't care about people like us. They'll lie and cheat no matter what to protect themselves. I don't trust anyone in positions of authority. Power leads to unhappiness, to corruption of the soul. Plato said that in *The Republic*. Something to that effect. I forget the specifics. Now I may not believe in souls, but I sure as shit believe in the very real and demonstrable fact that right now I discern a gang of corrupt mongers stepping between me and my hot fucking dinner."

"You could approach Manning yourself."

"I wouldn't touch that cretin with a yardstick. His inner core is the color of Rocky Mountain deershit. No way. Not a chance."

"You could hide somewhere, wait it out, and lie low till the dust settles. Maybe with Jim in the desert in Patagonia."

"Salter shoots. Salter doesn't hide."

"You could organize a counterinsurgency."

"Say more."

"You could backchannel him like he backchanneled you."

"I don't have contacts on the inside. I'm a solitary operative."

"You could follow him."

"I could follow him. Say more."

"Well, think of your grandmother. It'd be just like your grand-mother. That time in Santa Cruz. I forget the names. I'm sure it'd make her proud if you followed."

"That it would. Where is that cretin now?"

"He's leaving for New York soon with Franny."

"Why do I know that name?"

"She's my ex-girlfriend."

"Ouch. That's gotta sting, kid."

"I'm getting by okay. It was all too strange to be really mad about anyway."

"Forgiveness is overrated. It's so Christian. But I admire your position. You can trust that I'll be following her, too. Known asso-ciates of a given operative are to be treated just as seriously as the operative itself."

"I've never heard you use that word before."

"The circumstances demand bolder language. I won't let you down. What a spinning mess. What a bunch of malarkey. There are so many ways of seeing, kid. But maybe there are too many. I'm furious but I have to keep breathing. My first wife used to say that. She'd sit me down by the kitchen sink where I was drinking vodka and smoking hashish off a can of V8, and she'd tell me that it was important for me to keep breathing and drinking water and eating healthy foods and sheltering with my people. I'm a simple animal like any other, she said. We all have basic needs. Our desires are defined by lacks. I have to thank you for putting me up this river the way you have. The world is about to get batshit bonkers for me. I can just feel it. There's a stench in the air."

"I should be thanking you. You've taught me so much over these last four years. I don't know where I'd be without it."

"You're a whipsmart shooter, kid. But now I know you're more than that, too. You're a stir-crazy wardog just like me. I trust you'll go off and do unspeakable brazen feats with your life. Which brings us to the second item on the docket. Have you brought me prints for your final project? If I remember right, you were tasked with enlarging said snow shots to the size of a medium window, were you not?"

"That's right, and yes, I have. There are five variations in the series, though I'm now considering making it ten. Each variation has its own tones, its own ethos. I find myself favoring the deeper more saturated greyscales, but I go back and forth. I see them hanging in a room, the images the size of doors, lined up next to each other on the wall."

"I can't register sense perceptions below my sternum. You just hit me like a bullet. Let me sit here quietly and amuse myself with these. I can't believe what I'm seeing."

"Do you think they'll work?"

"I think they might make it hard for you to ever put down your camera again, but jeez, yeah, holy mother, these are the best shots I've seen in years at this lousy school."

"I appreciate you saying that."

"I can no longer feel my face, kid."

"What should I do now then?"

"Beats me. Probably you should start running somewhere to shoot, and not stop running until something forces you."

"Something like Take Creek, for example?"

"Well, maybe. Though it could be others, too. Take river. Take road. Take stream. Take path. Take trail. Take beach. Take heed. Take pause. Take time. Take breath. Take bus. Take plane. Take train. Take boat. Take pleasure. Take warning. Take hint. Take word. Take impression. Take in. Take out. Take with. Take to. Take along. Take away."

"There's the sense of an ending at play."

"That's fitting. But the shape of what's to come should be infinitely more exciting. Where's your first stop?"

"I have no idea."

"Not bad news for you, I think, surely. Wherever you go, just stay alert to the changing light. Take pictures of what you see there so that the rest of us can puzzle over what it might be like."

$$38$$

We arranged to meet near *Tunnels*, a foreboding earthwork at the far southeastern corner of campus. I brought a thermos of tea and a small bag of caramel cookies, arriving early and waiting in the grass. It was a lackluster day, gray and muggy. The sun was shrouded and socked in. Franny walked down the path out of the trees and waved. She had cut off her braids and foregone the usual Technicolor makeup. A mustardy, wide-wale corduroy jacket wrapped her shoulders like an old shorn blanket. She wore dark glasses with purple plastic frames. I stood up to greet her. Franny motioned for me to sit back down.

"There's no need for that," she said. "I just came to say bye. I wanted to say bye before I left."

"Here we are then," I said.

"We're here to say the word," she said.

I looked down and studied my shoes. I needed new laces, I realized, all of a sudden. The soles were wearing thin, a little smooth and far too sooty. A trail of red ants marched past me to oblivion. I could feel Franny watching me there from her perch.

"Rumor has it Annie Leibowitz is going to shoot Jillian Arcadia for the cover of *Artforum*," I said.

"That sounds like news in your world," Franny said.

"You have no idea."

"How is your world?" she said, looking somewhat concerned.

"Would you sit down?" I said. "You're making me nervous. Just take a seat on the grass. Sit by me."

"I'm okay here," she said.

"Okay," I said, looking back at the installation. "Maybe it's because this one's backdropped by the overcast sky and the sounds of the forest, but *Tunnels* is imbued with so much sadness, isn't it? I have to admit, I don't come here much. I don't really like it. I'm surprised this is the spot you chose to meet. It's an odd decision."

"It just came to me, I don't know."

"I brought tea," I said. "You love tea. You're not interested in having tea."

"I don't have time," Franny said. "We're leaving in a few minutes."

"New York City," I said, drawing out the words.

"I was offered a one-year fellowship with a really famous group. Zoe put in a word for me. I couldn't turn it down."

"Congratulations," I said. "I'm proud of you for saying yes."

Franny smiled but didn't blush. She rubbed at the side of her head. She almost seemed annoyed.

"And what about Manning?" I said.

"I'm not worried about Manning. He knows people. Manning will be just fine."

"Is he really as good as we thought?" I said.

"He's even better," Franny said.

"It's not a thing for me, you should know that. I'm excited about the future, too. You bet I am. I'm going on another road trip with Jersey. We're headed to Seattle, Portland, San Francisco, Los Angeles. After that, we're going to cross the border and travel around Mexico, just two friends on the road, with no timeframes, no fixed goals. Although that's not exactly true. We've talked about driving the length of the Americas to Tierra del Fuego. Jersey wants to climb in the Cordillera Blanca. I'm eager to get into ranching, maybe ranch-handing. I'd like to learn how to ride a horse."

Franny crossed her arms as if she were cold.

"I don't know what to say, or what I can say," she said. "I guess I'm sorry, is all."

"You don't have to do that," I said. "Really, you don't. Try to say something else. Make it a better version of yourself."

"Say something else, you're saying?"

"Tell me you've taken up baking."

"Baking?" Franny said.

"Sure, why not?" I said. "Tell me you're saving for a drift boat. Tell me you're becoming a communist, or an alcoholic, or a pedant, or a plumber, or a drupe farmer. Tell me something glowing. And please tell it to me abundantly."

"Dance," she said.

That was it. Just one word. A single syllable. She said the word dance and then she just went quiet. It seemed to say everything she wanted.

"I recently went to Commerce City," I said.

"I better get going," she said. "Tell Jersey I said bye, would you? Tell everyone bye for me."

I got up to give her a hug. Franny stepped back, walking away, fading quickly but then turning around.

I called out to her.

"It's just like you always said."

She nodded and kept walking.

I called out again, this time a little louder.

"You have a tendency to see things. You can render the form of certain events before they even happen. Are you listening, Franny? You're not like the rest of them. Don't let them beat it out of you."

Next day, I spent the morning hanging my work for an exhibition in The Media Annex. The pieces were heavy and difficult to handle on my own, not quite the size of doors as I had planned, but certainly cumbersome enough. I hung five prints on one wall and five on the opposite wall, as if the images were in conversation. When I was done, I put a chair in the center of the room and sat for a couple hours, deeply satisfied, surrounded by my work. Every ten minutes or so, a buzzer rang down the hall. I heard someone entering the room and coming up behind me. But no one was there.

I went to The Library to return all my books. Next, I dropped off lab equipment wherever it was necessary. I folded my linens to squares, per instructionals, and left them at the foot of the bed. After lunch, I picked up the mail and brought my towel to Laundry. Then I took my key fobs to Tech for data wipe and reprogramming. As I headed to The Admin to sign my final paperwork and approve my graduation, the sun popped out in this distended freakish mass and the clouds all burned away. People started coming out and talking in groups, filing out of the buildings into the hot heavy air. Hammocks were swinging left to right. Voices rose and fell, laughter in waves. The Wild Dogs charged up from behind a pair of dumpsters, and from who knows where before that, screaming and whistling, in white uniforms and black helmets with tinted visors, looking organized and purposive like never before. I leapt under a picnic table and covered my head, but a few of them saw me and grunted. Was that Peter? Or Margot? Or Maria? Or Todd? Or Gregor? Or someone else? Their faces were no longer recognizable. They ran over and spat on me as they passed, spit of tobacco, sour and pestilent, the stuff of the world, all so staining.

I caught up with Jersey later that day at The Rec, where he was in the throes of a high-intensity interval training circuit in the bouldering cave. I sat on the mat and watched him, amazed by what he was demanding from his body and what he could pull off now while hanging. We went for a stroll around campus and talked things through.

"Squamish is a town in British Columbia," Jersey said. "I'm meeting Holly there in a few weeks. Others are coming. Others by the thousands. I'm sorry we never had the chance to go out into nature like we'd hoped. Holly got busy. I got busy. Everyone's schedules, you know how it is. It's hard to carve out a window."

"I couldn't do it anyway," I said.

"I figured," he said.

"You were saying the town is called Squamish."

"Well, we're not exactly in Squamish, we're near Squamish. The climbing there is world–class. I plan to stay as long as the weather permits, probably until late September. Our camp invites people from all over the world. It's an idea. It's an experiment in right livelihoods. We climb. We cook. We sew. We play songs. We discuss issues. We set new routes. The idea's a communal arrangement."

"Sounds like Take Creek."

"Don't you dare say that."

"Maybe I'll come and visit."

"You should. This is the most technical attempt I've made so far. I'm going to climb until my hair falls out. That's my hope at least. After that who knows? I'm not all that preoccupied to be honest with you. It'll be productive for me to get away from raging so hard and burning stuff all the time."

"But the raging is one of your most admirable qualities," I said.

"Is not," Jersey said. "I've got my head up my ass, and it's been that way for years. I'm making the turn now toward Spirit. Anything could happen."

"I don't understand, Jersey."

"Me neither. That's okay by me."

"Are you still writing?"

"Meh, not so much," he said. "Mostly I'm just honing in on my body. Writing is always there, sculpture as well. But I barely finished my final project. I mean I barely eked it out. It's just horrible, too. I couldn't be less inspired. It's hard to imagine ever caring about art again like I once did. Somewhere along the way, I got broken."

"What broke you?" I said.

"I'm not sure," Jersey said. "But I shattered. That's all true."

"I guess climbing is much the same. It's an endeavor most people don't care about, which is maybe what makes it so liberating."

"Take an example. Do you like plants?"

"Of course," I said. "But not especially. Why do you ask?"

"Lucky you," Jersey said. "The known world doesn't care about plants, either. What good fortune for you if you happen to like plants then. What a lovely way to exist outside the norms of social practice. I say, the more esoteric the pursuit, the better. The less applicable to daily life, the better. I'm saying, go for it. I hope to someday have the nerve to make the transition to poetry. That's where the real freedom lies in waiting. Beyond poetry lie other adventures of course, but they're not for the weak of heart."

"I met with the Options Counselor last week," I said. "He told me his name was Jerry, but in fact, he was the same guy that interviewed me when Take Creek won its special accolade months back, and that guy was named Phil. Jerry slash Phil pretended like we'd never met."

"Best art school in the world," Jersey said. "Second to none."

"Jerry slash Phil says I'm hosed."

"I could come up with a theory about that."

"Jerry slash Phil says I should start crunching numbers."

"He's probably right, you know, as every pitch has its features," Jersey said, lingering in front of The Barn and a neighboring paddock that happened to be occupied by four goats. "But some pitches are worse," he added.

"Are you going to be okay?" I said, after we passed through a long silence.

"Meaning like physically or metaphysically or spiritually? Is there even a difference? I'm losing stride with differences. Climbing collapses most immediately recognizable differences. So does writing, but that's only because it heightens every particularity, and you forget how it even got started."

We kept walking, passing The Farley Gardens but never going in.

"The Wild Dogs have a similar effect on your average student," I said.

"That's so stupid, and so is everyone on the team," Jersey said.

"It took over. It spread like a fire in the wind. Soon there won't be anyone left that's not a Wild Dog."

"Who cares? Let's talk about Char. Where's Char in this moment?"

"Char is on the way back to Portland. They're heading home for a break."

"That's beautiful. Why can't I just be more like Char?"

"I'm going to see them this summer," I said.

"You'll be traveling then?" Jersey said.

We came upon a pair of hammocks strung in a stand of oak trees, shadowy giants shedding bark in strips and coils, the color of wet stone. We each hopped into a hammock and went slack. It seemed only natural, apropos of nothing, to just stop there on a whim and dangle one last time.

"I'll call you when I get there," Jersey said.

I asked was he talking Squamish or elsewhere. Jersey stuck out his hands palms up and shrugged.

"Wherever it is that I'm going," he said.

I smiled and told him I would do the same, and meant it, even though the sky was way too big then and I didn't yet know what it meant, what it meant to really call someone, and to really mean it when I called.

When I woke up a little while later, Jersey was gone. His hammock had been cut to pieces. The ends that remained flittered in the breeze like the torn flag of a defeated mountain army. Everything around me felt self-identical in that moment, everything save the sky itself, which spread out endlessly in waves, onrushing, the fleecy cloudscape, ever-bending and distorted. I lay there for an hour or so, until I felt mildly dizzy. Eventually I got up the nerve and started walking again. I went looking for photographs, perceiving distance in forward steps, in two pulls of cold water, a light snack, simple breathing, basic functions. shuttersnap. The days became weeks and then became more. I grew tired but kept walking.

IT WAS A MODEST room, an almost perfect square, with bare pearly walls and whatever else one was supposed to need in this place. There was a bed, a desk, a chair, a table, a blue milk crate, and a bag full of cameras. The metal shelves were all empty, dusty relics left to rot. In the corner of the room a hotplate sat on a cart. Next to the cart, a broken sink. There was no oven, no cabinets, no closet, no rugs. There was one lone electrical outlet hanging at the end of an exposed wire. Sunlight was scarce here, limited to a few hours a day, no more, seen briefly through the window that peered out on the adjacent building, brick by brick by brick. I saw myself around the room with a yellow plastic floor lamp over whose woven shade a thin fraying sheet was doubly draped. At least once a day, the lamp cut out and the room went completely black, and when the room did that, it tended to stay that way for two or three hours. The air at night was thick, tangy, stupid-quiet. It was easy to get lost in that, too. The sounds alone. The constant quiet. My phone kept dying for some unknown reason, and error messages became increasingly common. Every so often, the sound of the street rose between the buildings, like heat burning off the sidewalk. Down there, people were introducing themselves, talking out of turn, hollering, joining one another and forming crowds. I got in the habit of posing certain questions to myself—questions about what goes on down there? what sings? what bends? what bands together in the falling light?—that special variety of heedless, maniacal catechism that goes on for hours, maybe even years or a whole life.

One day, I was warming up a bowl of soup when the phone rang. Moments later, a distant bell tolled, stark and crisp in the night. The bell lingered in the wind, surging through the streets and up to where I stayed. The color of the lamp suddenly changed, flashing red. Emergency alerts started popping up on my computer. Notifications, updates, plans of action, procedures of public safety. These became the measure of our lives, like the waypoints in a new march toward madness. Noise was a form of meditation. Our lives had been reduced to mere calculus. I watched and listened, but wasn't afraid. I was just curious about what to do next. Like always, I sat in the room and studied the light, and then, quietly, carrying two cameras and with no particular destination in mind, I let myself out and walked off into the bluegreen night, and I didn't make it home for a long, long time.

ACKNOWLEDGEMENTS

A printed shoutout in singsong across the rooftops to everyone who supported me and my work. To my brilliant editor, Leland Cheuk, at 7.13 Books, for bringing this novel into the world. To my friend and cover designer, LA-based painter Madeleine Tonzi, whose colors and spirit built a home for the page. To fellow authors Sara Lippmann, Sharma Shields, and Beth Lisick: thank you for reading and shoring up my book with such generous, electric blurbs. To my publicist, poet Anna Zumbahlen: a bright and shining beacon for all things possible. I'm deeply grateful to my former teacher, author Jeremy N. Smith, whose integrity, humor, erudition, and unrelenting kindness ferried this young writer through a lot of long, hard years. A special nod, too, to author Nate Dern, for being my sounding board, an honorable old friend, and a long-distance advocate for me and my work. Thanks to all my fellow 7.13 authors, in particular, Jackson Bliss, Dionne Irving, Jenny Bhatt, and Ben Tanzer. To all my friends and family, old and new, who read my early drafts, always told me to keep going, and never once spoke a word telling me to quit. And to anyone else who I may be forgetting here, I thank you now, sincerely, for lending your hand.

ABOUT THE AUTHOR

Chris Rugeley was born in Houston, Texas, and grew up in Colorado. A graduate of the University of Montana, he worked as a bartender in San Francisco for over a decade while writing this book and earning his MA in philosophy from San Francisco State University. He currently lives with his wife in San Francisco and Northern New Mexico. *Take Creek, For Example* is his first novel.

Follow news, events, and updates about Chris and his work on Instagram @chrisrugeley and on his website at www. chrisrugeley.com.

9 798987 747100